Praise for *Natural Novel*

"Like Fernando Pessoa, Gospodinov has disappeared within his multiple selves (author, narrator, editor, gardener) and has become a detached observer of his own life. The narrative is rich in mini-stories . . . and the composition is multifaceted. . . . All this informs the postmodern quality of Gospodinov's fiction."

—*World Literature Today*

"*Natural Novel* is really an unidentified literary object and is almost impossible to retell. It is at the same time funny and erudite, arrogant and refined, yet brilliant in every respect and innovative in form."

—*Livre-Hebdo*

"The superb style and flowingly written narrative along with the clever switching between different forms of discourse and genres turn Gospodinov into a harbinger of a new, fruitful literary form."

—*Politika*

Georgi Gospodinov

NATURAL NOVEL

Translation by Zornitsa Hristova

Dalkey Archive Press

NORMAL · LONDON

Originally published in Bulgarian as *Estestven Roman* by Janet-45, 1999
Copyright © 1999 by Georgi Gospodinov
Translation copyright © 2005 by Zornitsa Hristova
French edition published as *Un roman naturel* by Éditions Phébus, 2002
This edition made through an arrangement with Éditions Phébus

Library of Congress Cataloging-in-Publication Data:

Gospodinov, Georgi, 1968-
  [Estestven roman. English]
  Natural novel / by Georgi Gospodinov ; translated from the Bulgarian
by Zornitsa Hristova.
    p. cm.
  ISBN 1-56478-376-6 (alk. paper)
   I. Hristova, Zornitsa. II. Title.

PG1038.17.O85E8413 2005
891.73'5—dc22

                              2004052738

Partially funded by a grant from the Illinois Arts Council, a state agency.

Dalkey Archive Press is a nonprofit organization located at Milner Library
(Illinois State University) and distributed in the UK by
Turnaround Publisher Services Ltd. (London).

www.centerforbookculture.org

Printed on permanent/durable acid-free paper and bound in the
United States of America.

"Natural history is nothing more than the nomination of the visible. Hence its apparent simplicity, and that air of naïveté it has from a distance, so simple does it appear and so obviously imposed by things themselves."

—Michel Foucault

NATURAL
NOVEL

1

There is always a long train of crying people and a shorter train of laughing people. Yet, there is a third train of people who no longer cry and no longer laugh. The saddest of the three. That's what I want to talk about.

We are getting a divorce.

I had a nightmare about what it would be like leaving. All our possessions are packed, cardboard boxes stacked to the ceiling, and yet the room still feels quite spacious. The hallway and the other rooms are filled with relatives—Emma's and mine. Whispering, rustling, and waiting to see what we're going to do. Emma and I are standing by the window. All that's left to do is divide a pile of record albums and we're done. Suddenly she takes the first LP out of its jacket and hurls it through the window. This one's mine, she says. The window is closed, yet the LP flies through it as if the glass were made of air. I take the next one out and hurl it too. Somewhere near the garbage cans it hits a filthy pigeon in mid-flight.

Everything happens in slow motion, which intensifies the horror. As the LP cuts through the pigeon's neck, there are several distinct short notes. The sharp bone of the pigeon's throat plays a few seconds from the track on the record. Just the opening tune. Some sort of cabaret song, I don't remember which one. 'The Umbrellas of Cherbourg'? 'Oh, Paris'?

'The Café with the Three Pigeons'? I don't remember. But there was definitely music. The severed head keeps flying (on momentum) a few yards further while the body tumbles to the ground around the garbage cans. There isn't any blood.

In the dream everything is simple. Emma bends down and hurls the next LP. Then I do. She does. I do. She does. Every LP repeats what happened to the first one. The sidewalk across the street is littered with bird heads, grey, identical, their eyes closed. With each severed head, the relatives behind us burst into enthusiastic applause. Mitza, our cat, stays by the window and salivates.

I woke up with a sore throat. At first I wanted to tell Emma about my dream, then changed my mind. It was just a dream.

2

The apocalypse may take place in one particular country.

I bought a rocking chair one Saturday in early January 1997. I had just got my paycheck and half of it went into buying that chair. It was the last one at the old, comparatively low prices. The incredible inflation that winter made the craziness of my purchase even worse. The chair was a wicker bamboo-imitation, not particularly heavy but large and difficult to carry. It was unthinkable to give up the other half of my salary for a taxi, so I hauled it like a basket-seller and started on my way home. I was walking, carrying the chair on my back and getting angry stares from passers-by for the luxury I had afforded myself. Someone has to describe the miserable winter of 1997, as well as all the other miseries—the winters of 1990 and 1992. I remember an elderly woman asking for half a lemon at the market. Others searched around the empty stalls at night for a potato that might have been accidentally dropped. More and more well-dressed people overcame their shame and reached into the garbage cans. Hungry dogs waited on the side or gathered in packs to attack pedestrians coming home late. As I write these fragmented sentences, I imagine big newspaper headlines in bold letters.

One night I came home and found that my apartment had been broken into. The only thing missing was the TV set. Strangely, my first concern was the rocking chair. It was still there. Perhaps they couldn't get it through the door—it was too big, I had moved it in through the window. I spent the whole night in the chair. When Emma came back, she tried calling the police. To no avail. Nobody paid attention to burglary calls anymore. Fuck it. I sat in the rocking chair, caressed my two cats that were scared by the mess (where were they hiding when the thieves came?) and smoked a cigarette over the ruins of whatever was left of my male dignity. I was unable to protect even Emma and the cats. I wrote a story.

An apartment is broken into. At the time of the burglary only the wife is home—fortyish, slightly fading, watching a soap opera on TV. The intruders—young, normal-looking guys—don't expect to find anybody there, but they quickly figure it out. The woman is frightened enough anyway. She takes the money out of the closet herself. She doesn't resist when they tell her to give them her jewelry. Wedding ring too? Yes, the wedding ring too. She removes it with great difficulty because it is stuck on her finger. Suddenly, when the thieves try to take away the TV set (the soap opera is still on, by the way), the woman puts her arms around it. She speaks for the first time, pleading that they take anything except the TV set. She just stands there with her back to the two men, clasping the screen to her breasts, ready to do anything to protect it. The thieves could easily push her aside, but they are surprised by her sudden reaction. She senses their hesitation and says ambivalently that they could do anything to her if they only leave the TV set alone.

The deal is struck. We'll fuck you, one of them says. She doesn't move. They quickly lift her skirt. No reaction. Her ass is still tight. The first one comes right away. The second takes more time. The woman holds on to the TV and doesn't move, only asks them to get on with it because her kids will soon be home from school. This, finally, discourages the second one and the men leave the apartment. The soap opera is over. Relieved, the woman lets go of the TV and heads for the bathroom.

How are the '90s going to end—as a thriller, a gangster movie, a black comedy, or a soap opera?

Editor's Note

Here's the story of this story.

As the editor at a literary newspaper in the capital I received a notebook. It was stashed in a self-made envelope addressed to me personally at the office. There was no return address, just smears of dry glue. Removing the notebook did little to relieve the sickness I already felt—approximately eighty crumpled sheets with tightly written lines on either side. Such manuscripts were never a good omen for an editor. Their authors, mostly elderly pests, drop by a couple of days later to ask if the work of their life—what else?—was accepted for publication. I knew from experience that if you didn't refuse them bluntly but, respecting their old age, kindly told them you hadn't finished reading it yet, they besieged you every week like weary warriors, determined to fight to the end. And though the end was near, the clatter of their canes on the office stairs often made me swear to myself.

Oddly, there was no title, nor an author's name. I put the notebook in my bag, planning to take a look at it when I got home. I could always reject it with the excuse that we accepted only typed texts and thus postpone the second visit by a few months. That night I naturally forgot about it, but in the next few days nobody showed up to seek an answer. I opened it a whole week later. As incredible as it sounds, it was one of the best things I had read since I became an editor. A certain man was trying to talk about his failed marriage and the novel (I don't know why exactly I decided it was a novel) was based on the impossibility of relating this failure. In fact the novel itself could hardly be summarized. I immediately published an excerpt and waited for the author to drop by. I had added in a little note that the manuscript had come in unsigned, probably due to the negligence of the author whom we would like to meet. A whole month passed. Nothing. I published a second excerpt. Then one day a youngish woman came into my office. She was furious that the newspaper was intruding into her private life. The woman wasn't a regular reader, but a friend had showed her the published excerpts. She claimed that they were written by her ex-husband who wanted to slander her. On top of it all the names were real, which, according to her friend, was reason enough for a lawsuit. All of a sudden the woman burst into tears, and then her anger subsided and she even looked kind of sweet. By fits and starts she told me that her husband was once a very decent man who wrote at odd times and even published a few short stories. Admittedly she never read them. He went nuts after the divorce. Now he had sunk to the status of a bum, loitering around the block to harass and discredit her.

'Would you show him to me?'

'No, you find him, he's always dragging his rocking chair around the local market. There's no mistaking him. And, please, don't publish this anymore, I can't stand it,' she said quite softly and left.

He made a living as all bums do, though he didn't rummage in garbage cans for food, or at least nobody saw him doing that. He'd get money by selling used paper for recycling. He was one of those quiet loonies. Hanging around the market, doing small favors, keeping an eye on the goods in the evening, which got him a few peppers, tomatoes, watermelons . . . whatever was in season. That much I got from the sellers after they repeatedly asked me if I were the police. They didn't know much.

I found him in the local park. He was rocking in his chair somewhat mechanically, as if he were in a trance. Matted hair, a long-discolored T-shirt and torn sneakers. Ah, yes, and a raw-boned street cat humped in his lap. He kept methodically stroking her. He couldn't be more than forty-five. They had warned me he hardly spoke, but I was a bearer of good news after all. I introduced myself. I think he smiled faintly without looking at me. I had brought the two issues with his excerpts. When I asked him if he was the author, he nodded without coming out of his trance. I tried to tell him how good the text was; I talked about publication and asked about other works. No effect. At last I took whatever money I had on me and gave it to him, saying this was his payment. He was obviously not used to earning money. For the first time since I got there he stirred, came out of his trance and looked at me.

'You're getting a divorce, right?' He sounded almost friendly, like someone offering his condolences.

Damn it, I didn't think it showed. In any case I looked

better than he did. I hadn't told any of my friends yet. A few days earlier my wife and I had filed for divorce. Since he had finally started talking, I asked him his name.

'Georgi Gospodinov.'

'That's *my* name,' I almost screamed.

'I know,' he shrugged, unmoved. 'I used to read your paper. I've met seven people with the same name besides you and me.'

He didn't say anything else. I left him there and hurried off. Everything unfolded like a bad serial novel. It occurred to me that I could call his wife and double-check the name. Before I turned the corner, I had to look back at him. He was still sitting there, rocking back and forth in his wicker chair. Like one of those plastic hands people used to stick to the rear windows of their cars, waving mechanically.

I returned a year later. In the meantime I had found a book publisher who liked the manuscript, so I only had to find the author and get him to sign the contract. I doubted I would be able to bring the man to the publisher, so I had brought the contract with me. It was late spring. I had already learned the name from his wife and had to swallow the coincidence. I felt a bit guilty for cringing that such a degenerate type could have the same name as mine. The publishing contract contained a decent advance that would surely do him good. I searched the local park, but he was nowhere to be found. I tried the market. I asked one of the grocers who looked familiar from my last visit. He didn't have a clue. My man was last seen sometime in October, no . . . maybe in early November. He didn't come anymore. Then the grocer shook his head and hinted, by the way, that last winter was bitter cold and the Wicker-Ticker (as he was known here) had planned to spend it in his rocking chair. During this time the man sold two kilograms of tomatoes, two kilograms of cucumbers and some green parsley, without missing a chance of praising his goods to me. All that—in a stale, somewhat screeching voice. I felt like crushing his tomatoes, one by one, plucking each leaf off his fresh parsley and sticking his head in the resulting purée. How come none of the grocers, the only people this bum seemed to talk to, hadn't done anything about him? Whatever, maybe get him a small room to spend the winter in, or even a basement . . . Yet my anger gradually subsided as it led straight to the question of why I, myself, hadn't done anything about the poor bugger. I left the market and found a bench in the park not far from the spot where last year I had my first and probably last talk with the man in the rocking chair. On top of it all, by a strange coincidence—because all coincidences always seem strange—we shared the same name. I told myself maybe it all turned out okay. Maybe the man pulled himself together, maybe the publication in my newspaper got him out of his chair and off to work somewhere; maybe he even started writing again, rented an apartment and found a new wife. For a while I tried to picture him in the living room of a condo, sitting in his rocking chair in front of the TV with slippered feet, old but clean pants and a warm sweater. And, in his lap, the same street cat he was stroking back then. The more I polished this picture in my mind, the less I could believe it. Finally I took out the publishing contract and did the last thing I could do for my namesake. I signed it.

3

*Atoms float in the void (the void does exist),
and by combining with each other they cause
things to appear, and by separating they cause
things to perish.*

Democritus (according to Aristotle)

Flaubert once dreamed of writing a book about nothing,
a book without content, 'a book that would be held together
by itself, by the internal force of its style just as the Earth is
suspended in the air without any support.' Proust has partly
achieved that goal using associative memory. But he too could
not resist the temptation of having content. My immodest
desire is to mold a novel of beginnings, a novel that keeps
starting, promising something, reaching page 17 and then
starting again. The idea or nucleus of this kind of novel can
be found in classical philosophy, and mostly in the naturphi-
losophical triad of Empedocles, Anaxagoras and Democritus.
The novel of beginnings would rest on those three pillars.
Empedocles insists on a limited number of arch-beginnings,
adding Love and Enmity to the four basic elements (Earth, Air,
Fire and Water) in order to start them moving and combining. The one closest to my novel is Anaxagoras. His idea of
panspermia, or the seeds of things (later Aristotle would call
them *homeomeria*, but this sounds nowhere near as warm
and personal), could turn into the impregnating force for
this novel. A novel created from countless tiny particles,

arch-substances, i.e., beginnings that fall into an unlimited number of combinations. If Anaxagoras claims that everything consists of tiny particles similar to one another, then a novel could indeed be built with beginnings only. Then I decided to try openings that had already acquired classical status. I would call them atoms, thus paying my debt to Democritus. An atomic novel of opening lines floating in the void. My first attempt went like this:

If you really want to hear about it, the first thing you'll probably want to know is where I was born, and what my lousy childhood was like, and how my parents were occupied and all before they had me, and all that David Copperfield kind of crap, but I don't feel like going into it, if you want to know the truth.

Whether I shall turn out to be the hero of my own life, or whether that station will be held by anybody else, these pages must show. To begin my life with the beginning of my life, I record that I was born (as I have been informed and believe) on a Friday, at twelve o'clock at night.

My name is Arthur Gordon Pym.

Squire Trelawney, Dr. Livesey, and the rest of these gentlemen having asked me to write down the whole particulars about Treasure Island, from the beginning to the end, keeping nothing back but the bearings of the island, and that only because there is still treasure not yet lifted, I take up my pen in the year of grace 17— , and go back to the time when my father kept the

'Admiral Benbow' inn, and the brown old seaman, with the sabre cut, first took up his lodging under our roof.

They helped Bai Ganio take down the cape from his shoulders; he donned a Belgian cloak—and everybody said he was now a true European.

'Why don't we all tell some story about Bai Ganio? Let's do it.' 'I'll tell an anecdote.' 'Wait, I know more . . .' 'No, me, you don't know anything . . .'

After much clamor we finally agreed that Stani would start. And so he began:

Immer fällt mir, wenn ich an den Indianer denke, der Türke ein; dies hat, so sonderbar es erscheinen mag, doch seine Berechtigung.

Eh bien, mon prince. Genes et Lucques ne sont plus que des apanges, des propriétés de la familie Bonaparte. Non, je vous previens, si vous ne me dîtes pas, que nous avons la guerre, si vous permettez encore de pallier toutes les infamies, toutes le atrocités de cet Antichrist (ma parole, j'y crois)—je ne vous connais plus, vous n'êtes plus mon ami, vous n'êtes plus mon "faithful slave," comme vous dites! Oh, hello, hello. Je vois que je vous fais peur, sit down and tell us about it.

The second day of Easter I was having lunch with Mr. Petko Rachev, a Bulgarian writer and journalist. He lived in a crammed two-story house on the corner of two narrow streets in one of the most uncivilized Istanbul areas, Balkapan Khan. Mrs. K., a relative of Mr. Rachev's who lived with him, placed before us *two big glasses, filled them with peeled sliced apples and poured on them black and delicious Palishman wine. We took the apple slices out with our fingers and sipped the wine, thereby continuing our conversation in a merry and contented manner.*

I was born in the year 1632, in the city of York, of a good family, though not of that country, my father being a foreigner of Bremen, who settled first at Hull. He got a good estate by merchandise and, leaving off his trade, lived afterward at York, from whence he had married my mother . . . I had two elder brothers, one of which was lieutenant-colonel to an English regiment of foot in Flanders, formerly commanded by the famous Colonel Lockhart, and was killed at the battle near Dunkirk against the Spaniards; what became of my second brother I never knew, any more than my father or mother did know what was become of me.

All happy families are alike; each unhappy family is unhappy in its own way. All was confusion in the Oblonsky's household.

That cool May evening chorbadji Marco, bare-headed, dressed in his robe, was having dinner with his offspring in the courtyard.

The dream of the Texas deer who's resting in its night shelter is disturbed by the clatter of horse hoofs. It doesn't leave its hiding, nor rises, because there are wild horses in the prairie too that wander in the night. The deer only raises its head, its antlers show over the high grass, and it listens carefully.

Separated like this, the openings acquire a life of their own and come together through intertextual similarities and contrasts just as Empedocles, Anaxagoras and Democritus had foreseen. If read quickly one after another, they merge and move like frames on a film reel, transfigured in a shared kinetic that kneads characters and events into some sort of new story. Salinger's opening, though disparaging of *David Copperfield*-type beginnings, flows smoothly into those particular lines by Dickens. Then the first sentence of *The Story of Arthur Gordon Pym* coldly introduces itself, only to fuse into the circumstantial story from *Treasure Island.* Then *Bai Ganio* smoothly tells the story of *Winnetou*, while the courteous French opening of the reception ball in *War and Peace* merrily flows into the ritual of an afternoon feast of Palishman wine and sliced apples at Mr. Petko Slaveikov's house. Like a story that's sprung from this conversation ensue the first lines of *Robinson Crusoe*, by the way, translated into Bulgarian by the same Mr. Petko. Somewhere around here the book decides to be a family novel and merges the Oblonsky family with that of chorbadji Marco without any qualms (why need there be any? one is Russian, the other pro-Russian) and anyway something goes wrong in both families, someone jumps the wall, be it Ivan Kralich or Anna Karenina. Even the Texas deer somewhere in the prairies is disturbed by the same noise. The world is one and the novel puts it together. The openings are already there, the combinations are endless. Every character is liberated from the predestination of his or her story. The first capital letters of the decapitated novels start floating like *panspermia* in the void, creating something new, don't they, Anaxagoras?

Or as Empedocles has put it so nicely, if a bit excessively, *from the earth rose many neckless heads, bare arms that swung to and fro, eyes with no foreheads above them floated around, trying to merge with each other . . .* From here on, everything can go in any direction. The headless horseman could arrive at Rostovi's reception and start cursing with the voice of Holden Caulfield. Other things could happen, too. Yet this Novel of Beginnings will describe nothing. It will only give the initial impetus and will subtly move into the shadow of the next opening, leaving the characters to connect as they may. That's what I would call a Natural Novel.

4

The divorce was neither long nor painful. The procedure didn't take more than four or five months, which was considered quite normal. Of course, we paid something to get it over quickly. I thought I wouldn't take it to heart. So did my wife. At the first hearing (which didn't last more than a couple of minutes) we testified that our decision was 'peremptory and irreversible.' The prosecutor was rude. She had hairy arms and a big mole on the left side of her nose. She set a date for the second hearing after a three-month reconciliatory period and called the next couple in. We decided to go for a walk.

'Well, you have enough time to decide before the next hearing,' my wife said. I was picturing all of our wedding guests now coming to the divorce. The two rituals are related, right? It would be appropriate to get the same witnesses now. At least this would save us the awkwardness of having to inform each one that we have broken up, that I no longer answer the same phone, etc. I also pictured our relatives crying at hearing us answer the judge with a 'peremptory and irreversible' *yes*. But they cried at the wedding, too.

'So, it turns out a marriage lasts between two yes's,' I said, avoiding her question.

My wife's pregnancy was already noticeable.

'Look, let's continue some other time. The final hearing is way off.'

00

'I was living with a girl who kept staying in the bathroom. At least four times a day for an hour and a half each. I've timed her. I waited like a dog in the hall and we talked. We had some very serious conversations like this. Sometimes when she fell silent, I looked through the keyhole.'

'The crapper is a rotten place!'

'Don't interrupt him; so what happened?'

'Nothing: we talked. As if she's locked herself in and you are trying to make her get out, thinking up anything to persuade her to unlock the door so you can finally see her face. Looking through the keyhole doesn't count; besides, sometimes she blocked it with toilet paper. But once when I was urging her to come out, she unlocked the door and told me to come in. It didn't work. The room is too small for two, you know. There she is, sitting with her panties down, looking sunk into the bowl with only her knees and feet sticking out. We couldn't have a decent conversation.'

'You were disgusted, weren't you?'

'I told you. The crapper is a rotten place!'

'No . . . It wasn't that. It just didn't work. It wasn't smelly.

Well, not much.'

'Wait . . . That's it. That's the heart of the matter. If you can stand the stench of your girlfriend shitting in front of you, if you're not disgusted, if you accept it like your own smell, 'cause you don't mind your own (do you?), then you stay with that woman. Get it? Call it the great love, one and only, Miss Right, the one you can stay with for at least a few years, etc. That's it. These things don't happen often. Just once, and that's the test.'

'Cheers! Have you patented those things or are you trying out your next novel on the present audience?'

'No, I'm serious, but the test might be different for jerks like you. Cheers!'

'Enough about bathrooms, please. We're at a table, eating, drinking, and then suddenly all those toilets and smells . . .'

'No, wait a minute. Why shouldn't people talk about toilets at the table, huh? Why do you go to the bathroom? Because you've been at the table, stuffing your face, eating and drinking, and then you rush to the bathroom. That's natural, isn't it? Yet you're telling me it's not natural to talk about it at the table. Now listen: is there anything closer to the toilet bowl than the bowl that's on the table? They're both called bowls. And both are porcelain. Porcelain bowwww-wwwls! I've thought about those things and I tell you there's plenty in common. You must be fucking stupid not to see how important the toilet is. You know what I'll do one day? I'll collect all toilet stories, I'll put them in order, I'll add commentaries and indexes and I'll publish a *Great History of the Toilet* . . .'

'Paperback, printed on toilet paper.'

'Good idea. But the history will be divided in two. The house toilet is fundamentally different from the public toilet. And I'll tell you what the difference is.'

'Can I finish my livers first? 'Cause soon everything will get disgusting.'

'The big difference is that when you go to the public toilet it's only a procedure for you. You close the door, you unzip your fly, do it, pull your pants up, and leave. Everything is done as quickly as possible.'

'Because the toilets are shit.'

'Maybe so. But that's the procedure. But in your toilet at home you can go at any time, even if you don't need to. You can stay for hours, read a book or read cartoons. You can simply rest your chin on the palm of your hand and think. No other room gives you such privacy. This is the most important room, you know. The most important room.'

'So, when you go in the public john it's a procedure, and when you shit at home it's a ritual.'

'Yeah, something like that. Those are private rituals, for your eyes only. Because nobody sees you there. I don't think even God looks at you.'

'That's why I tell you the crapper is a rotten place. Some grandfather of mine hanged himself in the outhouse. He took his belt off and slid it over a beam under the roof tiles. He put his feet in the hole so he could hang down. His trousers had fallen to his ankles because they were too loose without the belt.'

'When I was a kid, I went to the village movie theater and wondered why nobody in movies went to the toilet. All those Indians, cowboys, entire Roman legions, and no one took a shit or peed. While I ran to the john after only two hours in the theater, those guys from the movies never went there in their whole life. See, I told myself, real men don't squat with their warm asses; I had decided to try to see how long I could go without defecating. I held it in for three days. My stomach hurt like hell, I was walking slightly bent; my parents got scared and were about to call the doctor. On the third night, I gave up. I locked myself in the bathroom and let go. I felt like an untied balloon that deflates, whooses and flaps until there's nothing left of it. That's when I started not believing in movies. There was something wrong about them, something . . . unrealistic.'

'That's just because you've been watching stupid films. You can judge a movie by its toilet-shyness. Remember how in *Pulp Fiction* Bruce Willis goes back to get his watch and decides to toast Pop-Tarts, while Travolta is reading in the john? When Travolta comes out, the toaster clicks, and Bruce Willis jumps and shoots him. So the toaster pulls the trigger and the kitchen blows up the ass of the toilet. See how it fits?'

'How about the cop in *Reservoir Dogs*, Mr. Orange was it? the one that told the story about drugs in the john with all the details added to make it believable? When he was making his story up, his boss told him: you've only got to remember the details. That's what will make them believe you. The action, he says, takes place in the men's room. You've got to know everything about that john. Paper towels or a dryer, what kind of soap, and so on. Whether it smells a lot or whether some son of a bitch shit all over one of the stalls . . . Everything.'

'I think I am going to throw up . . .'

5

Plant Weddings
Linnaeus

My wife's pregnancy was already noticeable. This seemingly innocent phrase has a darker side if I told you (how shall I put it?) that I wasn't the author of her pregnancy. Someone else was the father, but I was still her husband. The pregnancy did her good, giving a certain ease to her movements and a nice curve to her otherwise bony shoulders.

I was walking her home after the final hearing for our divorce. What do people do on such occasions? A few days earlier I had rented an apartment in the area and Emma had the insane idea to get photographed together for one last time. Just like a wedding. We entered the first studio we came across. The photographer was one of those sweet old talkative guys who always need to know what the occasion is. "A family photo, eh?" as if this determined the right positioning. He took his time arranging us, slung my hand first around her shoulders, then in hers, turned our faces towards each other, looked through the eyepiece, then came back again. At last a click, a downpour of wishes for a happy and large family (yes, obviously the pregnancy did show), and we were free to go.

00

'The greatest thing about the '90s is still that dive down the dirtiest Scottish toilet in *Trainspotting*.'

'What about Fassbinder's films, or Antonioni's—always an important toilet scene. Or Kusturica, with that ridiculous suicide attempt in the toilet. I think it was *When Father Was Away on Business*. The guy hung himself on the tank above the toilet but flushed instead of dying.'

'I don't like Kusturica. Boring slob. A moody Balkan sentimentalist.'

'Okay, then forget about Kusturica. See how Nadya Auerman poses before Helmut Newton on the toilet bowl, while Naomi Campbell gulps down another beer, squatting there with her panties warming her ankles. On the cover of her album. Makes you want to be reincarnated as a toilet bowl.'

'A year ago there was a symposium of owners of Asian public toilets and field experts in Hong Kong. I read about it in a newspaper. You know what kind of papers were presented? Something like "Practical Measures for Eliminating Bad Odors" or "Historical Developments of Public Toilets in the Guangzhou Province." But the best one was

"An Analysis of Civil Satisfaction in the Public Toilets in the Republic of Korea." I must have put up that newspaper clip somewhere.'

'A friend of mine went to Beijing and told us about the airport toilets. A big hall divided into cells with four-foot partitions (you know how short the Chinese are) and no ceilings. You squat in your cell, completely exposed above the waist, with two polite Chinese guys nodding and smiling on either side. Right below is a gutter which, if you look closely, features the excrement of everybody on your left.'

'We had the same toilets in the army. Just thinking about them makes my eyes hurt. We had to pour chloric acid in them for disinfecting. Makes you blind in no time. The latrines were the old soldiers' responsibility and when they wanted to harass us, they made one of us clean them. One guy decided to pay them back by stealing a pound of yeast from the kitchen and dumping it down the hole. You should have seen that pus swell and spill!'

'I saw something funny on a toilet wall in Berlin. "Eat shit. Millions of flies can't be wrong." In German, of course.'

'More sauce, anyone?'

'Toilet graffiti will have its own chapter in *The History* . . . Why does the toilet induce the urge to write? Most of those writers hardly have the urge any other time. I'm sure they never wrote a single line on paper. The toilet wall, however, is a special kind of medium. Publishing there brings different pleasures. What if being on your own triggers secret mechanisms, the primal instinct of writing, of leaving a sign? I wouldn't be surprised if all those cave drawings were scraped while primitive man was squatting over his warm turds.'

'But that's difficult to prove because excrement is perishable, with a short period of decomposition.'

'Still it would be nice to look closer at the area around the cave drawings. But let's get back to toilet graffiti. The most isolated and lonely place on earth is actually quite public. Once you could read anti-government slogans there. The courage of society was displayed on the toilet wall.'

'Intimate toilet revolutions. Some courage, some society. Look at them, shitting out of fear and then scribbling "Fuck Todor Zhivkov" and "Screw the Communists" on the walls. Forget that crap. All our bed-wetting dissidents are like that. The only public place these people protested in were the public toilets.'

'Loud standing ovations.'

'I've seen a wall that read: Don't push yourself, we don't have any standards here.'

'Ok, what did I say? The toilets are the only surveillance-free space. A real utopia where power is absent, everybody is equal and everybody can do what he wants under the pretext of doing what he came for. A feeling of absolute impunity. You can't get it anywhere else, just the grave and the toilet. The interesting thing about it is that both are about equally large. On the other hand, all that calls . . .'

'*The calls of nature as calls for freedom.* Now *there's* a title for a thesis.'

'Hold it . . . all those slogans on the toilet walls could be completely apolitical. Maybe it's only language rioting. It's not just your body with its lower depths entering the toilet, it's language as well. Language also feels the urge to unbutton its trousers, to let go, to blurt everything pent-up that fucking day, the whole shitty life. All those stupid fairy-tales, stupid newspapers, stupid people you meet, so when you are finally alone in the toilet you feel a rightful urge to write "Fuck" on the wall. This is language's urination and intestinal relief.'

'So when we're talking about toilets, we're talking about language.'

'The food is getting cold and I have to go home. And when my wife asks me what the hell we talked about, I'll tell her—we talked shit.'

'You said it! Mr. Queasy! Guys, a toast to him. I think this is a revelation.'

6

I wish somebody had said: This novel's good, because everything is uncertain in it.

He woke up late the next day. He hadn't cleaned up after last night. The ashtrays stank like dormant volcanoes, if volcanoes had a stench. Last night he was drinking with three of his friends who had helped him move to his house. They spent the night talking about toilets. He pushed the conversation in that direction himself. This suited everyone best. Nobody wanted to talk about what had happened. Nobody said a word about it. The best way to liven up a conversation is to try avoiding a certain subject. He got out of bed . . . in fact he had slept fully dressed on a mattress on the floor. He headed for the bathroom, tripped over a stack of books and started swearing. When will he put all that stuff in order—cardboard boxes, bags of books, a still-unassembled bed, an old typewriter and all the other bits and pieces like that? Ah, yes, and a disproportionately large wicker rocking chair that takes up half the room and lends a decadent finesse to the whole chaos. On the way back from the bathroom he carefully evaded the cardboard boxes piled up in the corridor, but once in the room, his head hit the rather low-hung lampshade inherited from the last tenants. He collapsed in his chair and for the first time in a couple of days considered the situation. It seemed like only yesterday he had everything—a large apartment in one of the best parts of town, a telephone, two cats, a decent job, a couple of family friends who often came by. Oh, yes, and a wife. Though the last few months they communicated only when they had guests, she was the force that kept their home in order. Peace and quiet, and he only had to find the time to write. All that had ended in a couple of days. The collapse had in fact started at least a year earlier, but with some masochistic pleasure they both ignored it. He got up and took a pack of cigarettes out of the precious rations in his travel bag. They had used up everything last night. At thirty he didn't exactly want to start all over. Starting over. What a dumb phrase, fit for second-rate novels and box-office hits. 'Turn your back on all that.' 'Get up and fight.' 'Rise up for a new beginning.' Bullshit.

So where do you start? What kind of start is that anyway? Going back five years . . . No, five were not enough. Ten, fifteen . . . Everything started a whole lot earlier.

It was almost lunchtime. He had several options. Screw everything and go to another city, or another country. Hang himself on the tank above the toilet. Take all his money, buy five packs of cigarettes and just as many bottles of brandy, lock the door and wait for death. Go out for a sandwich and a large coffee.

Fifteen minutes later he decided to start with the last one.

7

In the temple of that rose
a black beetle took the vows.

How can a novel be possible these days, when we no longer have a sense of the tragic? How can even the idea of a novel be possible when the sublime is gone and all we have is everyday life—in all its predictability, or worse, in the unbearable mystery of destructive chance? The daily grind in all its mediocrity—but only here do we get a glimpse of the tragic and the sublime. The mediocrity of everyday life.

Once, when time moved more slowly and the world was still enchanted, I heard or made up the following magical formula: if you pluck a horsetail hair and soak it in water for forty days, it will turn into a snake. Lacking a horse, I tried a donkey hair. I don't remember if I waited the whole forty days or whether the hair turned into a snake—maybe not, since the tail wasn't equine.

Anyway, I discovered that the idea of the magical only had to spend a minute in my head to turn all donkey asses into magnificent Gorgons. I had read about the Gorgon in an illustrated volume of Greek mythology. I wrote it down in a calligraphy notebook with a Levski print on the cover. This was the first miracle nature had offered me, the first everyday miracle. What would I do if ass rumps had stayed ass rumps and that was it? As I see them now in their disenchanted state. Anyway, it's been a long time since I last saw an ass rump.

We could mention here that even in ancient times Epicurus and his student Lucretuis insisted on the natural autogenesis of living organisms under the influence of dampness and sunshine.

If ontogenesis really imitates philogenesis, i.e., if human life does repeat all the centuries from the beginning of nature, then childhood took place somewhere between the seventeenth and the eighteenth centuries. At least regarding the loving attitude towards that same nature. Linnaeus, he who like a new Adam gave names to the plants and introduced binary nomenclature, the so-called *nomina trivialia,* named one of his early writings *Introduction to Vegetable Engagements* (written in the early eighteenth century yet published as late as 1909). Here's a description of pollination that could well belong to Hans Christian Andersen:

The petals of the flower contribute nothing to reproduction; they only serve as a nuptial bed so splendidly arranged and so preciously scented by the Great Creator himself to let the groom with his bride celebrate their wedding with utmost magnificence. When the bed is done the time comes for the groom to embrace his darling bride and pour himself inside her . . .

8

Sub rosa dictum.

I'm pregnant, my wife said that night. That's all. Films and books offer two types of response to such an announcement:

1) The man is surprised but happy. He looks silly, goes to her and puts his arms around her. Carefully, so he won't harm the baby. He doesn't know it's still a handful of cells. Sometimes he presses his ear to his wife's belly: it's too early for kicking. A close shot of the woman's eyes, deep and moist, already maternal;

2) The man is unpleasantly surprised. We've felt there was something wrong about him from the beginning of the novel and now, in the moment of revelation, his whole hypocrisy shows up as obvious as the blue line on a pregnancy test. He doesn't do a good job of disguising his displeasure. He doesn't want this child. He lies to his wife. The woman's eyes in a close-up.

So, Emma came home, sat against me without taking her coat off and said, 'I'm pregnant.' She didn't need to specify who the father was. We hadn't had sex for about six months. She said only 'I'm pregnant,' thereby erasing the above two variants. I couldn't think of how to react. I didn't remember ever reading about such a situation. Learning that your wife is pregnant with another man's child happens once in a lifetime, no, once in a couple of lifetimes. You jump to your feet, you swear, kick the table over, and break her favorite vase. The moment must be made use of. Outside lightning flashes, a thunderstorm's approaching. The world cannot stay indifferent at such a time. But no, nothing of the sort. I tried to light a cigarette very slowly. I didn't know what to say. My wife seemed confused by my silence and blurted out that she'd seen the baby on ultrasound and it was tiny, just half an inch long.

I admitted I didn't know what to say. I was surprised at not feeling any hate or any jealousy. How can you react to the unthinkable? What can you do?

She said she wanted to keep the baby and me.

I stayed with Emma for two more months.

The baby got three or four inches long.

Every day I said a mental goodbye to her, to the cats and to my room.

Two months when nobody made a decision.

With every new day your wife turns into a mom, and you cannot be the father of her child.

9

Towards a Natural History of the Toilet

Where does a story start? What do people say at the very beginning? Shall we start with wrath, as Homer did? Or shall we start with names? If Plato was right in *Cratillus* that there is an innate rightness of names for both Greeks and barbarians, then we have to start here.

Going back to the history of the word 'toilet,' we come to the English 'closet,' and then we find the Latin *claudo*, *clausis*, which from its very first meanings insists on closing and locking the door. Other meanings of the verb have a conclusive connotation—a closing-off activity. It also means hiding, secluding. The Romans had a knack of saying everything with one word. So the toilet was the place where you locked yourself up, finished whatever you came for and then covered your tracks. Indeed the Romans didn't specify what exactly one did there. It could've been anything. In Ephesus, for example (what is this city doing now in Turkey!), you can see a well-preserved Roman toilet. Vast, marble-seated, and completely unpartitioned. It's right next to the public baths, with something like a covered bridge between them. After bathing, the Romans would spend the whole afternoon in casual conversation on these marble seats. Memento! I forgot something. Of course they didn't immediately place their warm bodies on the cold marble—they let the bare asses of their slaves warm up the stone.

But back to names. Don't you think that the Bulgarian word *kenef* ('toilet') sounds better in this part of the world? It wasn't coined by bums, as many worthy citizens think. It comes from the Old Arabic *kaniph* and denotes *what is hidden from the eye.* It rings true because it came to us through Turkish or because it somehow suits our latrines best. If we open the Naiden Gerov six-volume dictionary we will find a name that is even more precise and uneuphemistic. Late nineteenth-century Bulgarian boldly calls the place 'nuzhdnik' (*need*nik') and 'sernik' (*shit*nik'). At the end of this century my grandfather calls it the same, without having read Naiden Gerov. He still can't imagine having your toilet inside the house, right next to the kitchen. 'Going outside' is much more decorous. That's another phrase, as literal as it is euphemistic. Outside, somewhere in the backyard—the inveterate patent of his generation. In fact every male has experienced that watery copulation with nature every time he's pulled off to the side of the road. In the bush, or over virginal snow where you could even drip-paint something vaguely resembling the late Picasso.

Or maybe we should start with a date, a notch in time, a number. In 1855, England saw the invention of the first underground public lavatory, or water closet. Men only. Perhaps assuming such needs in the ladies showed lack of refinement, to say the least. Although it was below ground level, the running-water facility was not the least bit rundown. It was prestigiously and lavishly tiled and brassed, with heavy oak doors, something like a pub, except you're pissing out the liquid instead of taking it in. From those times dated this ode to Thomas Crapper, the inventor of the water closet, written by an anonymous, relieved user. It goes like this:

> *Crapper's invention*
> *Is well worth the mention*
> *No need to blush—*
> *Here comes the flush!*

How far can you go into history? Can it tell private stories, everyday experiences, like Duret did in his *Wondrous History of Plants*? Aldrovandi in *The History of Snakes and Dragons* and Jonston in his *Natural History of Quadruples*—they did just that. Natural history, especially the one we know from the sixteenth and seventeenth centuries, has no scruples about its field. Thus Aldrovandi's history includes etymology, structure, sustenance, reproduction, tropes and traps, allegories and mysteries, emblems and symbols, legends and hearsay, dreams and cooking recipes.

Occasionally we hear strange stories and rumors about toilets. A couple of years ago the newspapers told the story of the Swede who found a boa in his toilet. The man went to the smallest room in his house and was just about to sit down when he saw something move beneath him, coiled in a spiral—a real boa. History keeps silent about what happened next—whether the Swede was bitten or whether he automatically flushed.

The fact is that similar rumors appear sporadically. The

toilet, although it has been cultivated into something pleasant, is still connected with the underground world.

The '30s saw the rumor that the New York sewage system was full of alligators. And why? A certain family went to Florida on vacation and brought back two baby gators. When they got bored with them, they flushed them down the toilet. The reptiles, however, didn't give up but instead fed off dead rats and sewage and even reproduced, to the horror of New Yorkers. Even later denials in serious publications like the *New York Times* only convinced the citizens more that the New York underworld was a downright jungle. I don't know whether there was anything to it, but I personally know an old lady who swore she saw a garter-snake slide down the spout when she turned on the tap. It's only a matter of size.

Of course our talk about toilets we had at the table will also enter my natural history. *Sine qua non.* All kinds of stories go there, even the most trivial ones, especially the trivial ones. Like the story of my friend Wensel, told by him personally:

'I went to a university washroom. One of those unisex ones. Splashed with shit. And I'm not a student, so I *do* mind. That's when I heard a knock on the door and I said it was occupied. A fantastic female voice answered, "Sorry." A gorgeous sexy voice, I tell you. I was dumbstruck. And wondering how I could get out of this mess, so that this girl won't think it was me who crapped there when she came in. So I stayed there—I was done but I didn't know how to get out. If I stayed long enough, she might leave. But if she stayed, the whole plan would backfire. That's enough time to crap all over the place. There's no proving it wasn't me. So what if I was even wearing a bow tie and carrying a leather bag? For her I would be nothing but a champion shitter. Tricky business, the whole system of public toilets is awful, with no way out, not even a fucking window. The bow tie even makes you look more like a pervert in that crappy context. Makes you an idiot. Meanwhile the girl outside is waiting and surely getting mad. Then I made a decision. I took the bow tie off, crammed it in my pocket, unbuttoned my shirt, flung the jacket over my arm and rolled up my sleeves. I became invisible, part and parcel of this miserable washroom. I still think this is the best strategy in such situations.'

'I kicked the door and went out.'

10

Nobody has seen it, but still it exists . . .

After the wedding we lived at Emma's place for a few years. Her parents' place, actually. Emma was on rather strained terms with her parents and my arrival only made things worse. The apartment was too small for two families. We lived in a small bedroom with a balcony, so the only places we would bump into her parents were the kitchen and the bathroom. My wife would seize the chance, while her parents were watching TV, to cook a quick supper, which she then brought to our room. The other hot spot was the bathroom. I got the knack of sensing when someone was getting ready to take a shower or use the toilet. I suppose Emma's father also made an effort to avoid me, because we managed to spend a couple of months without seeing each other. We were more likely to meet in town (where we just nodded formally) than in those 70 square meters we inhabited. I don't remember having any arguments with him—small wonder, since we never talked. But I still can't say how the tension piled up the way it did. Mutual antipathy, just like its opposite, has no need for excuses. In fact excuses would only ease the tension, but we carefully avoided them. Four years later, when my wife and I were finally living on our own, the tension stayed with us. That's the most amazing thing about it. Her parents were gone to a new apartment at the other end of town and we controlled the recently forbidden realms of the kitchen and the living room. I could go to the toilet at will and stay as long as I pleased. And still the tension haunted the place. I had the feeling it had oozed into the furniture, the wallpaper and the carpeting. Emma and I started fighting incessantly. It just happened, I can't remember any particular reason. As if everything pent up in that small room had now found release. Emma's relationship with her father was strangely mirrored in her relationship with me. I felt I was going insane. We changed the wallpaper, threw away the two old armchairs and rearranged the rooms beyond recognition. I didn't tell Emma what drove my enthusiasm, but I think she sensed it. Nothing helped. There was a flawless, indestructible mechanism that never failed to spoil everything.

The short stories I wrote back then (I had found a second-rate magazine with a first-rate budget and published under a penname for a handsome fee) got increasingly paranoid. One of them, called 'The Mechanism,' was about an old press that used to print a not-very-popular daily newspaper dedicated to criminal stories and paranormal phenomena. The newspaper went bankrupt and the machine was put away in a storehouse. A month later the newspaper surprisingly came out on the market again. Nobody knew who was publishing it. The former editors didn't have a clue. The strangest thing about it was that the news was covered one day in advance, so you could read what would happen tomorrow. All forthcoming murders, rapes and accidents were described in minute detail. It finally turned out that behind all that was the same press. It had printed the newspaper for so long and lived on its ink and blood that even though the people were gone, it kept working with terrifying momentum.

What was the mechanism that spoiled my marriage with Emma? I'll never forgive myself for staying in that place, though I doubt that moving out of the apartment would've solved the problem. Things had gone too far. We slept in separate rooms. Each morning we took care not to run into each other on our way to the bathroom. The same old story. I knew it was getting to Emma, too, but neither of us could do anything about it. The mechanism was working.

11

I'm thinking about a novel of verbs and verbs only. No explanations, no descriptions. Only the verb is honest, accurate and aloof. The beginning took me three nights. I chain-smoked and didn't write anything. Which verb should go first? Each one looked weak and inadequate. You can't start with 'deliver,' because 'conceive' must precede it, and 'copulate' comes even earlier, and before that comes 'desire' and so on, all the way back to another 'deliver,' a crazy vicious circle. Verbs on every level—a circulation of liquids inside the organism, an oscillation of cell membranes, verbs in the alveoli.

I'm sure a verb started it all. It couldn't be otherwise. I got up. Lit a cigarette. Walked to the window. My wife came in. Going to bed? No.

She shrugged and left. I thought of her getting into her half of the bed, the two cats sliding under the blanket with her.

12

Only the banal stirs my interest. Nothing else amuses me so.

The more irrationally isolated I became about my marriage—that is, talking about it—the more I drifted towards the bathroom. Only in that place, in that room, and in that language of toilets could I relax.

I buried myself in all kinds of research to find with some wicked satisfaction how shyly—or shall I say queasily—the toilet was always excluded. Language avoided the subject. No science explored it, no discipline claimed it. I decided to look it up as a partition of space, as an architectural element, as a building. I read everything about civil engineering. All I found was a meagre couple of lines somewhere at the end of the otherwise circumstantial chapters on country and urban housing, on downtown and uptown areas, on public services and water-supply systems. And that was it. I started reading everything with the toilet in mind and annexing all sorts of tidbits to my topic, even if their ostensible meaning was elsewhere. As Garfinkle was surveying *The Routine Grounds of Everyday Activities* or when sociology was discussing the banal in our daily life, I secretly rejoiced because that was my subject precisely. I loved reading Schütz who claimed to study the world of immediate social experience (*die Sociale Umwelt*) where 'we share with our closest people not just the periods of time but a sector of our spatial world that is commonly accessible. Thus the other person's body is within my range, and vice versa.' Wasn't Schütz talking about that very place? Wasn't the toilet part of the primeval ground (*Urgrund*) of the unquestionably given that must now be questioned and subjected to interrogation?

Schütz was appointed grand master of the new science whose primary subject would be the toilet. Another invitation was issued to Lyotard, who was searching for the '*oikeion,*' that shadowy space of privacy and solitude that counterbalances the *politikon*. Well, I knew the answer to his prayers.

In the 1930s Ortega y Gasset complained that the walls had soaked up the anonymous noise of the plaza and the boulevard. I could offer him the quietest and most secluded place in the house. The last haven of civilization. I saw myself as a new Virgil waiting to lead those people to the circles of domestic paradise.

13

Carlson? Wasn't he a good-natured pedophile?

'When women overeat, their tummies swell and they lay babies'—that's how children explain nature.

I love to talk with them seriously, as if they were adults. Actually I find adults boring. We started light-heartedly.

'Do you know who lays the eggs?'

'Hens do. They don't lay cows or clocks.'

'Who lays the hen then?'

'Well . . . the tree'—what an easy escape from the vicious circle of the paradox, what an easy change of species.

'Who lays the tree then?'

'The seed.' Aha, he's learned his lesson here. Slightly disappointed, I decide to bluff.

'The seed? How could a seed that small lay a tree so big?'

'Well . . .' Pondering the question for over a minute, baffled by my remark. Normally big things give birth to smaller ones, and here . . . 'Well . . . the roots then!'

'And who laid the roots?'

'Thunderbolts,' he says with lightning speed. 'They fall into the ground and they become roots.'

I give up. I never thought of the shared rhizome of the thunderbolt and the root.

Half an hour later I try the young physiologist again.
'Have you ever seen a beetle?'
'Yes, the beetle is what bites the ladybugs.'
'So that's where the dots are from . . .'
'Only it's not dots but holes.'

14

The fly. The fly is the only creature God has allowed to haunt dreams. She alone is admitted by the Creator into the realm of the sleeper. She alone can cross the impermeable membrane between the two worlds. In that she is a tiny likeness of Charon—if we assume that sleep is a little death. It's hard to gauge how the fly deserved this faculty. Oh Lord, what if she is Thy Angel in disguise, so when we shoo it away in disgust or, Heaven forbid, squash it between the palms of our hands, we are committing a mortal sin? (Here readers are requested to say a prayer and ask for forgiveness, just in case.)

It's also hard to determine how exactly the fly enters the dream. We shall never know whether nostrils, ears or other hidden apertures are her gates of choice.

And yet I would advise you to lie down in the afternoon, when flies are buzzing around the room, and try to drift off. You will seem to stop hearing them, but pay attention to a few details in your dream—the noise of a passing chariot, the lovely voice of a benevolent lady or the drizzling of rain from clear skies. The fly will be waving the baton.

15

God was fine milk and melting . . .

Nobody has ever succeeded in transporting something from his dream. On the way out of dreamland there's an invisible customs-house where everything is confiscated. I was a kid when I first noticed the thin barrier where That Thing stood. I called it That Thing because I had no name for it. That Thing searched me thoroughly on my way out of sleep and only let me wake up when it had made sure I wasn't smuggling anything. Sometimes I dreamt of the local confectionery for days, or rather nights, on end. I waited in line and when it was my turn to face the salesgirl, I started rummaging through my clothes and my terror grew with each searched pocket. I had forgotten my money again. It was there, in day territory, in the pocket of the trousers I had taken off for the night. So shame and horror were all that was left from my dream. That and the taste of untouched pastries.

One night I took all my savings with me. With the money from the piggy bank they amounted to the considerable sum of two leva and twenty to thirty stotinki. I put them in my pajama pocket and I was off. Off to sleep, that is. I think That Thing didn't search me on the way in. I stood before the salesgirl, clutching the money in my pocket. I wanted to impress her by pouring a handful of coins into the saucer so I could 'contemplate' her. I don't know where I had heard that word but I persisted in using it as a synonym of 'woo.' The smaller the coins I gave to the salesgirl, the longer I got to contemplate her. I splurged on several butter-rose petit fours, some muffins, two bottles of millet-ale and a handful of toffees. I didn't want to eat them on the spot. I put everything in a bag and I patiently waited to wake up. In the morning my bed was empty. I searched the pocket of my pajamas. The coins were there. It was That Thing at the customs-house again, the thing which gobbles up the best memories from your dreams. I have heard people calling it the Itslippedmymind. Maybe that was its name.

16

*A certain Mr. Knaute froze a few frogs; they
became fragile and broke easily; yet he took
the unbroken ones to a warm room and seven
to eight hours later they melted and became
fully alive.*

Priroda Magazine, 1904

When I was nine, God came to me disguised as a light-
bulb. That's how it happened. I was on a school trip to Sofia.
After the zoo we were taken to the Alexander Nevski Cathedral, maybe because we were close and it was starting to
rain. They told us that what we were about to enter was not
a church but a 'temple monument.' We understood only the
second half of that strange combination but somehow didn't
imagine monuments to be like this. It was really impressive
inside and we were wary of getting lost. While we were waiting for the others to come out, a crippled old man came to us
and started telling us about God. The more loud-mouthed
kids immediately informed him that God didn't exist, or
Gagarin and the other astronauts would have met him long
ago. The old man just shook his head and said God was like
electricity—it exists but you cannot see it, it flows and makes
everything work. Shortly afterwards, the teachers came out
and took us away from the old man. But his words made
us think. God and electricity were equally vague to us, yet
I immediately blurted out to the teacher that God lived in
lightbulbs. There was another school trip the next year; this

time to the biggest water power station in the country, for educational purposes. We were shown huge coils, gears and motors and we were told that this was where electricity came from. The teacher took me aside and asked whether I still believed in that rubbish about God and electricity. I was a big boy now so I said no. And yet, at home I was always extra careful when I turned on the lamp or the hotplate. God blinded and scorched.

A great time for empiricism. As high school students we had heard that human urine was particularly medicinal and drinking it could cure all kinds of diseases. It seems the rumor hit the grapevine hard because our biology teacher (that robust blonde whose crossed legs thrilled the virgin souls of us in the first row of desks), got mad at the innuendo one day in class and took to weeding it out so disgustedly you would think somebody had offered her the remedy. Which only proved that this urine theory thing was not so bogus after all, or what was the fuss about? The next day three or four of us had already tried the liquid (need I say that your future naturalist was one of them) and described its taste as not particularly nasty, slightly salty and sour like sea water according to some sources or like pickle juice according to others. We knew that uric acid was the reason. Never again did we taste life so intimately as we did in childhood when every rumor was unflinchingly tried.

17

What happened to that photograph of me and Emma taken on the day of our divorce? Did anyone collect it from the old guy at the studio?

Or have I quite consciously misplaced it among meticulously bound old newspapers to make sure I never find it? That's what people do with photographs they take at funerals, as well as with the dead themselves. They tuck them away somewhere at the far end of town or in a special sector of their not particularly reliable memories.

There comes a point when people start losing their desire to have their picture taken, or they only do it under special lighting.

My wife had the strange hobby of collecting photos from weddings and funerals. She kept them together, which seemed sacrilegious at the time. Now it doesn't. You open the drawer and by the sweetly grinning faces of the newlyweds you glimpse the waxy stiff jaws of the deceased. But all photos had flowers. Lots of them. Mostly the same ones—from all-purpose carnations and various kinds of roses to the cheaper wild flower bouquets and hastily picked dahlias and lilac branches from somebody's garden. The foreground of one funeral photo was adorned by several magnificent callas, 'the bridal flower,' as my grandma called it. The mourners looked like strange black-clad wedding guests. Somewhere behind them lurked the village band. The band for weddings and funerals. Looking into the photos, I knew why people didn't like keeping funeral pictures. The camera is unforgiving. When the photographer had been noticed, the mourners posed, as if they were about to smile.

Dividing the pictures of me and Emma together was the hardest thing to do.

Here we are in the very beginning of our relationship. Sometime in our sophomore year. Strolling along Shipka St. by the Doctor's Garden. Emma, I and Vesso, the eternal trinity. For a year people were wondering which one was dating her. Each of us is awkwardly caught in mid-movement. Were we really so happy? I don't remember who took the photo.

Here we are at a party: Vesso, Emma, I and . . . Sanya, with whom I split up just a few months earlier. Sanya was one of those women who try to get close to your new girlfriend. She'd hung on to Emma who had naively invited her to party with us. In another photo, taken perhaps three or four hours later, somebody (might well be me) had registered the two of them dancing cheek to cheek. In fact 'cheek' is not the right word. A foot shorter and generously endowed (our bosom friend, as we used to joke), Sanya was virtually glued to Emma. The photo clearly showed the fingers of her left hand clutching the ass of my future wife. Was she taking revenge or did her lust, as I'd always suspected, extend to women? I almost got worried for Emma. In my fear I used up a lot of film. I don't remember the three of us ever getting together after that evening. I suppose the two of them didn't either.

Ah, here's the wedding series at last. Emma is looking even taller and slimmer than usual in a simple tight-fitting dress complemented by long gloves and a veil. I'm wearing a toxic-green suit that's too big for me. Both mothers are weeping. Today, now that the marriage is over, their tears seem justified. Emma's father is missing from the picture. Well, he was missing from the wedding, too. In the last moment somebody dragged an uncle beside her mother so she wouldn't look like a widow.

The seven years of our marriage are painstakingly documented. Plenty of friends and parties. In reality there are never as many as there seems to be in the pictures.

I skip two more albums with similar photos; time and again the occasional new face, otherwise the crowd remains the same.

And here I am alone at last. On the bank of the Danube, in Sremski Karlovtsi, Yugoslavia. There was a peculiar kind of pleasure in being alone in a strange place, on the streets of a strange city, in a country where you don't know anyone and you're certain that nobody knows you. Here I am in Novi Sad, sitting in a street café in front of the cathedral square. All former Austro-Hungarian states have one. Naturally, at the other end of the square is a McDonald's. The square and the café are full of young people. Gorgeous women, teenagers, young girls with roller-skates. You are distinctly aware that nothing will happen between you and any of the women at the nearby tables. And romance is all that matters to you in the long run. Because you are a lunatic who purports to be a writer and all the pretty women around you are nothing but a future story. That's why you're going to sit alone, pampered by the waitresses. No wonder: you keep ordering to prolong your stay at the café. At last you will take a 'final' walk around the already empty square, you'll have a quick Big Mac and go back to your hotel room. The only thing you'll write in your notebook tonight will be the sentence you saw sprayed on the back of the cathedral: 'Opium forever!' And that will be all that you accomplish.

A cold breeze is wafting in from the river. Probably there is some Danubian Europe, a utopian state unlike any other part of the continent. An integral space where the waltz and the salon coexist with the boat and the fishermen village. Where the steps of 'The Blue Danube Waltz' intertwine with the raw rhythm of 'The Serene White Danube.' Where local reasons (of the general sentimental variety) prompt college girls to throw themselves in the Danube so the river transports drowned bodies from Schwarzwald to the Black Sea. Where the water is dirty and the catfish are always larger than the small boats.

The Kinks used to sing, 'People take pictures of each other / Just to prove that they really existed.'

18

A List of Pleasures in the 1960s
(Birth to 2 years)

. . . The pleasure of floating in the womb, your first and only nursery . . . of peeing in your own diapers . . . the pleasure of what's warm and damp . . . then clean and dry . . . the pleasure from mother's breasts . . . and generic pleasures of my parents: Elvis Presley, Gina Lolobrigida, dinner at a Bulgarian restaurant in Sofia, movies at the village theater, a pack of Sun filter cigarettes, romantic French films . . .

19

I knew a man—kind, quiet and thoroughly deserving of everybody's good feelings—except for one unfortunate habit. He liked to belch after a good meal. He did it spontaneously and said he felt an urge to do so, and that it was one of the few pleasures he had in this life. He rarely had company for lunch. One day he read that the people in the Orient not only belched on a regular basis but even considered it a sign of good manners. My acquaintance then packed his things and said something that earned him the reputation of a smart and sensible man. He said that people who turn their pleasure into a form of good manners know the difference between what is pleasure and what is good manners. And, with a final belch, he turned and left for the Orient.

Another friend of mine had the reputation as a great seducer. Women were to him what alcohol, work or drugs are for others. He devoted all his time to them. In the rare cases when he was womanless for a couple of days he claimed withdrawal symptoms, he was nauseated, grew pale and sank into the deepest depression I had ever seen. He kept a map of

Bulgaria over his bed, with flags marking each of his intimate venues. The map bristled like a hedgehog. He had only a few mountain towns left. After each conquest he summoned me to his place, poured two glasses of anisette (he considered anisette a strong aphrodisiac and drank nothing else) and told me the history of his conquests in great detail. I had the feeling he did it all for the sake of description. Then he took a new flag and slowly pierced the next town, the way you pierce a rare specimen in a herbarium.

The ending was banal, as with most stories that start out well. One day, in a moment of insanity, my confirmed bachelor friend got married unexpectedly. 'I got flagged,' he smiled sadly on the rare occasions when he could get out. Nothing was left of the great conqueror, the taxidermist of women. Nothing but the stories. He asked me to pick out a town, be it Elhovo, Sopot or Rousse, and recalled that particular story once more. Alive as ever.

Both stories are made up, of course. Although to me they sound real enough. I'm sitting in my room, making up stories and trying to be cheerful. Why am I doing all this? Why am I trying to write a Natural Novel? So I can forget a certain woman? So I can remember how I used to live? There's a reassuring lot of geography in these histories.

20

A List of Pleasures in the 1970s
(3 to 12 years)

. . . The first pleasure of language, of babbling, 'He's alive, he's alive' by heart . . . first introduction to my brother, a blond baby, entrusted to my other grandma . . . the first squiggly letters (my handwriting has hardly evolved since) in the margins of childrens' poetry books . . . the pleasure of writing my own name . . . the first infatuation with one of my cousins . . . the pleasure of playing doctor with her . . . the pleasure of the first serious book, the only one my grandparents owned: *Notes on the Bulgarian Uprisings*—a huge, brown hardcover, the first 60 pages were missing . . . 'Pants down' by my father's command . . . watching cowboy (East German) movies, 'Uncle Goika, Uncle Goika, he's behind you!' . . . the first dirty song:

> Mungo Jerry
> Is newly married
> She scrambles the eggs
> He scrambles the beds

. . . playing spin the bottle in the dark . . . my first story . . . sweet things, syrupy sponge cake, baklava, butter-nose toppings . . . getting my first poem published . . .

21

They say I'd been enamored. Who hasn't been enamored . . .

Philodemus, first century B.C.

Everything started on 4 May 18—.

Here's a possible beginning for a mid-nineteenth-century novel. It makes me feel good when somebody knows the precise date of the beginning. On the fourth of May. Not a day earlier, not a day later. OK, and what happened on the third of May? On the second? On the same date in 17—.

And so, I found out on the fourth of May, but I still can't say whether that was the beginning or the end. My wife came home from work a little after 8 P.M. I was watching the news. She didn't take off her shoes and jacket. Outside a cold May rain was falling. She collapsed in the armchair, the two cats immediately snuggled next to her, and she said it. She didn't say it loud; she seemed to be speaking to the cats . . .

Many years ago I found the courage to write in a letter something I had never dared tell a girl. I remember that the sensitive nature of the letter had prompted me to use a green pen. 'Everything can be written in green pencil,' Kharms says. I was in the final year of high school and I had firmly chosen this girl to be the only woman in my life. A long week of feverish expectation. When I got the answer, I didn't dare read it immediately. I didn't open the envelope until the evening of the next day. Inside was a single sentence: 'I love you as a brother and something more.' I was confused and no good at the interpretation of such feelings. I phoned a female friend who seemed far more experienced. She told me that to be loved as a brother was a catastrophe, but the second part of the sentence—'and something more'—gave serious hopes. I clutched at that 'something more.' When I opened the letter a second time, however, and I looked more carefully at the words . . . my God . . . I had misread a few letters. The phrase was actually 'and nothing more.' No chance at all. I remember my throat got instantly sore, my temperature rose and all my energy seemed to drain. I stayed in bed for three days. As they used to write in the nineteenth century—something broke deep inside me. Nothing after that would seem so tragic and important.

22

A List of Pleasures in the 1980s

. . . I can't remember any pleasures.

23

Italy? Where they all wear boots and eat frogs . . .

When I was in seventh grade, one of my classmates refused to join the Komsomol and once during recess we were summoned to the vice-principal's office—me as the class president. The sun was shining through the sheer curtain and glowing in the ashtray on the bureau where the clean-shaven, nicked-throated vice-principal was smoking a Stewardess. We all feared him more than we feared the principal, just as the lieutenant-colonel is dreaded more than the colonel. When this scrawny man stood before us (we were both half a foot taller than him), I panicked that he wouldn't recognize us and would start slapping me. He, however, had decided to try the nice approach. Here's the conversation, or shall I say the interrogation, as it stands in my memory.

'Let's see, who doesn't want to be a member?'

'Me,' said my classmate Krasyo.

'So you don't want to join the Komsomol?'

Krasyo said nothing.

'Would you tell me why?'

Krasyo kept silent and looked to the side.

'Why doesn't he want to be a member?' He was asking

me this time. My turn to say nothing. I really didn't know. I was sure Krasyo didn't know either. When admitted, you were normally asked, 'Why do you want to be a member of the Komsomol?' There was an official answer to that and we knew it, but this was the first time we heard the opposite question. I was trying to use a technique of 'transposition.' I fixed my gaze on something in the room and tried to transport myself there. I'm not in the room anymore, I'm that fly down on the windowsill over there and nobody notices me. I have no other goal but to walk the pane. And I do it diligently.

'Perhaps you've made up your mind to leave the country?' To Krasyo again, sarcastically. A positive answer was out of the question.

Just then Krasyo hesitantly answered 'yes.'

I remember how I switched back from flyhood and how I was sure we were about to be slapped. But the vice-principal was so surprised that his voice went falsetto.

'And where do you choose to go?'

'To Italy,' Krasyo answered almost in jest, or so I thought. Then the slapping began. I saw the vice-principal stand on his toes to hit us. Two slaps each. It didn't matter who was planning to escape and who wasn't.

'*Where* will you emigrate? To Italy?' he answered himself and added: 'So you can listen to ABBA, huh?'

I sensed that Krasyo was opening his mouth to explain to the vice-principal his mistake when the bell rang and saved us.

Only later did we learn that his daughter had immigrated to Italy two years ago and he would never be a principal.

'How did you pick the country,' I teased Krasyo later.
'I was just joking,' he said. And he shook with laughter.
But we both knew that recess was over.

And still Italy was appealing. It sounded soft and lustrous, with lots of vowels and a sliding 'l'. I-T-A-L-Y. Seven years after the slaps I went there for a couple of days. At the age of twenty, on my first trip outside the country, I ended up in Venice. I walked the streets with a notebook, trying to record everything I saw.

24

Let's talk about something else. Football? Tarantino? Dogs? Cats would be better. I prefer them to dogs. Cats never go in packs. There's nothing I pity more than stray dogs and cats. They've got it even worse than the homeless. And still I pity felines more. Dogs have learned a few tricks. They've picked up after the beggars, successfully copying their sympathy-inducing behavior. They approach you with feigned innocence, wistful eyes, they get hit by cars, smashed on the asphalt or crippled. Their misery stares you in the face.

Stray cats have a different kind of pride. They avoid closeness and hide their misfortune, creeping into basements or under parked cars. They don't count on our sympathy. I've heard that even domestic cats, sensing their time was up, run away from home or find some nook where they could be alone in their agony.

Emma and I had two cats—Mitza and Patzo. Mitza was a Siamese with glass-blue eyes. We courteously called her 'the hyacinth kitten.' She was a baby when a friend gave her to us. I took a week off work so I could feed and cuddle her.

Small kittens need cuddling more than they need milk. Our friend, who got her as a present, had heard some scary stories about Siamese cats gnawing their owner's throats at night. He just wanted to get rid of her. Mitza didn't have any teeth yet. She slept in our bed, between me and my wife. I often found them hugging each other in the morning. Annie, our friends' five-year-old daughter, used to say that 'Emma's born herself a kitten.' One of our cat-breeding manuals said that felines tolerate their owners but rarely get attached to them. Mitza was separated from her mother too early to remember her so I suppose she took us for guardians of her own species who obstinately tried to walk on their hind paws. The desire to own a cat was differently motivated but equally infantile in me and Emma. I admit that for me the cat was more of an affection, something like the pipe and rocking chair that every self-respecting writer has. I had already acquired the latter two. I saw myself sitting in the chair in a housecoat and slippers, a pipe between my teeth and a warm electric body purring faithfully in my lap. I must have seen that picture somewhere.

For Emma the cat was the minimum condition for feeling like a mother. She talked to her, cuddled her and brought her up like a child. Sometimes Emma herself looked like an overgrown kid lost in her game. Too late did I find that inside this game was another in which Emma was trying to show me how much she longed for a baby. Our marriage had already started cracking and I stubbornly claimed that I didn't want any children while our relationship was so undecided. With every argument the cat cringed on the windowsill, staring at us wildly and hissing. Books describe this condition as typical anxiety neurosis. We knew a couple who had several cats that threw themselves from their ninth-floor balcony. They got divorced some time later. Ours was a very humane divorce. It saved a couple of cats.

Mitza was all right, though, because our apartment was on the first floor. We found Patzo two years later. Somebody had dumped a whole litter of cats in the basement. All night long we heard distant sounds of mewing that grew weaker and weaker. We searched around the building for hours until we found where the sound was coming from. Only one kitten had survived. A few nights later Patzo perked up and started venturing out of his box. The Siamese bared her teeth immediately. She had never shown such aggression. Her body stiffened, her hair bristled and she growled so fiercely that the sounds choked and suffocated her. Meanwhile the kitten naively approached and sniffed her, as if he'd found his mother. For several months Patzo lived in a separate room and cried for the Siamese. And then Mitza felt a gush of some maternal feeling and went to the kitten herself. She licked him, cared for him and let him play with her luxurious tail. And so the two cats who couldn't bear to be in the same room didn't stray to more than a muzzle's length from each other. My marriage with Emma was going in just the opposite direction.

25

The white rose has always been a symbol of silence and discretion. When there were confidential and very personal talks to be had, the room was adorned with white roses. To this day people use the expression 'said under a rose.' *Sub rosa dictum*.

The clover is the emblem of Ireland.

The leek is the emblem of Wales.

The emblem of Japan is the chrysanthemum.

The thistle became the emblem of Scotland after a curious incident. Once, when the Danish decided to attack the Scottish army, a soldier stepped on one of the many thistles on the coasts of Scotland and screamed in pain. The Scots heard him and forever banished the Danish. From there on they have honored thistles as their national emblem.

And the rue (*Ruta graveolens*) is famous as the model for the club symbol in a deck of cards.

The Guide to Amateur Gardening, 1913

26

One must never eat fish before he's two, lest he grow mute.

(I forget where this comes from.)

We realize it too late, after we have been seduced. It would be easiest to call it 'The Big Seducer Up There.' I would accept that, if we agree that by 'God' we mean 'language.' Not 'the Word' but 'language.' In fact He (God or language) spoke for a mere six days . . . On the sixth day He uttered 'Man' as his final word. He never spoke again. All kinds of words have been attributed to him, but I don't think He said them. Because He doesn't communicate with words, He creates with words. The things this Language has uttered materialize in the moment of their articulation. Nobody else has attained such language. And many have tried. The Bible is an anthology of such attempts. That's why I call the study of God philology. What would happen if somebody did achieve God's language (the tautology is inevitable)? I made up the story of one such man and I was overcome with fear.

A man appears who had mastered the Language, the Language of those six days. When he says *water*, an ocean opens before him, when he says *night*, instantly the day gives way to darkness, when he says *woman*, she's right there beside him. Such language needs open spaces, a void. Being already articulated, this world proves too narrow for the language of the newcomer, too fragile for his imagination. The whole history of the world depends on what he'll say. The newcomer can hardly bear the responsibility weighing upon him. He shuts up and keeps to himself. He struggles to stay awake lest he mumble in his sleep something that could delete the world in a flash. What would happen if the words *fire, ashes and ice, apocalypse* slipped from his tongue? My wife asked what would happen if the man just stumbles and swears? And she burst into laughter. You're right, I told her, but it's not funny at all—and I shuddered. As a man.

I didn't know how to finish this story. One way was to have terrified friends pull his tongue out, but I didn't think that would help. So I chose the other ending, which seemed more natural and reliable. Everything lasted for six days. On the seventh day the man realized that he had lost the Language.

And he sat down to rest.

27

Sclerosis will make us new people. Old jokes will always be funny.

I had been dead for a few hours. That's exactly how my wife put it. I don't remember anything. She'd come home from work and found me in the rocking chair, as usual. I was looking strange, my mouth half-open and drooling. She could have spared me the last detail. She'd talked to me, called my name—nothing. Then she shook me hard. I'd given her a confused look, *you didn't recognize me, do you get it?; Madam, you're not my mother*, I had said, *her I remember.* Nothing, I don't remember anything. Just then the doorbell rang. I heard it and walked to the door. I had come to my senses, my wife said. I was fine. Just a little headache. I really couldn't remember the last few hours. Must have been fatigue. A temporary breakdown.

'You must see a doctor,' my wife said. 'A . . . neurologist.' I'm sure her first thought was 'psychiatrist.'

'Yes,' I told her.

Of course I would see no doctor. If I had what I was afraid I had, doctors could do nothing to help me. One of my aunts had Alzheimer's. They poisoned her with drugs and they kept telling her family to put her in a psychiatric ward. That's what they called the madhouse. She did go to one shortly before she died. In her rare moments of clarity she cried like a little girl begging her parents to take her home from camp. She complained they soaked her with cold water, that they gave her electric shocks. No, I won't give up so easy. The latent period of this malady is long. I can live as a normal man some more. On the other hand, it could have really been fatigue. I only had to slow down a bit. I would leave work if I had to, I'd search for something else. Still, on the next evening I dug out letters from my cousin who regularly wrote to me about her mother's illness. Ten years ago. I skipped everything else and read only the passages on Alzheimer's.

'. . . A friend, an evangelist, told me that only the Virgin Mary could help my mother now. Not the Son and not the Father, can you imagine? . . . Morning and night I pray to the Virgin to save Mom. I know you don't believe in these things, but we have tried everything, everything. We already lock her in. She managed to get out a few times and walked the streets, no instinct for self-preservation at all. She got lost, half-naked. At times she comes to her senses, remembers who I am, hugs me and cries. Then she can't recognize me again. She forgot Papa first. She yelled she couldn't sleep with a strange man. She begged me to let her visit her mother, though you know Grandma died 15 years ago. I feel like the mother of my own mother. I let her cry, sometimes I scold her like a child. I avoid looking at her face, because I don't want to remember her like this. I just don't want to remember her like this . . .'

I'll never get that far. Never. Never. Never. Never. Never.

28

Smoke gets in your eyes . . .

If someone asks me what I did last year, I can safely answer that I smoked. Nothing was granted as much diligence as cigarettes. Going out was down to a minimum. My work permitted it. I rarely answered the phone. I stayed home with the cats and smoked. From time to time an old acquaintance would visit; she was a terrible addict. Just out of rehab, she claimed she was clean but nobody would hire her. I don't think she insisted much. She borrowed small sums of money from me and never paid them back. On the other hand, she always offered me a joint. Perhaps she thought she was paying back the loans. For her, drugs were more valuable than money. She said that in the West dope was not considered a drug. She told me how she once tried some forest mushrooms that where much stronger than heroin.

When you take a bite, Hasha told me (I don't know whether the nickname was derived from her name Hristina or from hashish, but who cares), you see all kinds of elves, gnomes, spirits and fairies. Sometimes you can even see Queen Mab herself. Those mushrooms make you see things that are otherwise invisible, but exist.

I liked the mushroom story, but I stayed with cigarettes. I've always felt some guilt towards Hasha. We started smoking together in high school. She went further. I don't know whether she's given up 'mushrooms,' but I'm sure she lived with elves. She made me feel like a schoolboy who ran from class along with everyone else but came back at the last moment. Others would say I was saved. I thought Hasha looked pretty saved to me. Two years earlier she had started talking about emigrating to Israel. When I asked her about it, she always gave me the same answer: "I'm in Jerusalem already." And she must have been, while I never left the living room of our apartment at the periphery of Sofia.

My father's ashtray is Finnish, with a lid. It looks a bit like a little cask with a single-cigarette indentation. I always liked the idea of a personal ashtray, as personal as only a toothbrush and a razor can be. Some completely unfamiliar letters are engraved on the side of the ashtray (my father didn't know what they meant either). Much later, when somebody translated them for me, I was struck by their bluntness: 'Everything is ashes.'

When I smoke, I unconsciously copy my father's gestures. The energetic tapping of the index finger on the cigarette, the knit brow as you suck on it, all the concentration and importance of the gestures. The hardest thing to learn was the natural slight bending of the index and middle fingers. Mine were always artificially straight.

While I was browsing an illustrated pre-war magazine, I came across a short article about some guy who smoked a record number of cigarettes per day. When they asked him why he used matches instead of the newly fashionable lighters, he said he didn't want to spoil his teeth with the burnt gases from the lighter. The true smoker is an aesthete who takes care of his teeth.

Well then, I didn't want any more from life than to be sitting in the backyard of some house among nettle and hemlock, sinking in my rocking chair with a pack of cheap cigarettes, inhaling everything with the smoke: clouds, roof-tiles, airplanes, the Milky Way, everything. You can swallow anything with a bit of smoke. I wanted to feel the smoke get into my lungs, and come out pale blue and exhausted.

There is something angelic to ending up like this, dying as you smoke one cigarette after another very slowly in the backyard of a house. In the urn of a special ashtray, for you and you only; that's where one day they will find your ashes. And nothing else. Nothing they can hold on to, no body, no stained fingers, corroded lungs or decayed teeth. Just some ashes. If you are the perfect smoker, there will be no ashes, either. Fade into thin air . . . Now that I think of it, didn't the words on that ashtray say that 'everything is smoke'? There's more hope in that. And more ecology.

29

Towards a Natural History of Flies

Flies are dipterous insects with a pair of well developed front wings. Most flies have lived around Man since the beginning of time and are therefore called synanthropic (*syn* means *with*, *together*; *anthropos* means *man*). They dwell in a man's house, around his excrement, on landfills, etc. We can thus assume that the typical synanthropic flies we know today have been involuntarily created by man. Or by his waste activities. Some scientists argue that flies have existed long before Man and were even then feeding on corpses and excrement. But even they don't deny that once Man came onstage, flies readily recognized him as their host and importunately entered his home. Ever since then, the host won't welcome his pestilent guests, although they want no more than the crumbs off his table, and thinks up all sorts of contraptions to chase them away. He nails plastic curtains over the door to keep them out; puts a piece of rubber on a stick to hit them; fills platefuls of vinegar to drown them; or catches them with his hand and encloses them in matchboxes. Small kids practice something even more effective: capturing a fly and tearing off both wings which immediately excommunicates it from its dipterous order and turns it into an infantry creature meant to scare and warn off other flies. People practice all of the above (thankfully with little success) for no other reason than their ignorance of the true significance and possible usefulness of the fly.

First, the fly is a reducer, i.e., an organism that decomposes complicated organic matter—corpses, offal, carrion or excrement—to inorganic matter that can be used by the plants again. Thus the ordinary fly *Musca domestica* or the lavatory *Eristalis tenax*, and even the Bluebottle fly *Musca vomitoria* serve as a natural restriction of a raging organic revolution.

The body structure of dipterous insects and flies in particular is quite curious. The fly's eye is a true revelation. It is well developed and covers most of the head. In fact the eye consists of thousands of tiny eyes, hexagonal facets, each slightly protruding. Every facet can perceive just one pixel of the picture, whereas the whole image is formed in the brain. Therefore the fly sees the world as mosaic, or multi-angled. It is commonly believed that flies are nearsighted, but what more detailed, indeed minute perception can we imagine? The fragmentation used by some novelists as a literary device is in fact borrowed from the fly's eye. What kind of novel would we get if a fly could write a story . . .

What kind of novel would it be? Of course, I don't doubt the fact that it has a language, which naturally is different from ours. As I am the one currently interested in the fly (why isn't the fly interested in me?), I have to discover the mechanism of its language. As far as I know, the language of bees has something to do with the figures they draw with their flight. The same analogy could be sought with flies. The domestic fly is closest to people, it is always at hand. I said 'at hand' out of habit. That's how Man has communicated with them for all time. When we are looking for a new language, we should avoid inertia, that's why we'll keep flies not at hand, but at eye level. The next stage in the investigation of this language can be named the ability to converse with one fly only. This would require daily observation of a single specimen. Every fly has its idiosyncratic flight, i.e., language. Some flies are more loquacious and circle in the air longer; others speak slowly, alight in mid-sentence, go back to the beginning and forget their point. It would be wise to look for flies with a clear and legible flight that do not decorate their stories too much and know where to stop. All flies look the same to the ignorant. If the person who has set to educate himself by learning this foreign language disregards the aforementioned stage of concentrated observation of a single fly, he would often fail to identify the different specimens and would constantly buzz from one story into another.

30

When ashes are sprinkled on a dead fly, it rises up, experiences a second birth, and starts life afresh.

Lucian, *The Fly, An Appreciation*

Lately I've been occupied with something that might seem strange and maybe symptomatic. I've been studying flies . . . and, frankly, their stories. Fortunately, the object of my observation is always right before my eyes. Right before everybody's eyes as well, and therefore invisible to them.

And why this sudden interest in flies? I'm trying to convince myself it's for the novel I'm writing. A multi-angled novel, like a fly's way of seeing. A novel full of details, matters small and invisible to the naked eye. A novel as banal as flies. See, I tell myself, that's why I need flies. Those insects that buzz above us, sleeping on the ceiling or strolling along on our tables; living and reproducing in decaying bodies and outhouses.

They and they alone are capable of connecting the ether to the chthonic realm of the toilet. The fly is the mediator of the world, the angel and the devil in one. What better model to base a novel on, what better allegory! Or, as Plato says in *Ion*: 'For the poet is a light and winged and holy thing, and there is no invention in him until he has been inspired and is out of his senses, and the mind is no longer in him.'

Like a crazed fly. We know that Plato was never particularly fond of poets.

In the ideal novel individual episodes will be held together by the trajectory of a fly. I will say it again—the thread of the story will be the trajectory of a fly.

And again: a fly.

A fly. Af-ly. A fl-eye. A fly. A fly. A fly. A fly. A fly. A fly. A fly. A fly. A fly. A fly. A fly. A fly. A fly. A fly. A fly. A fly.

OK, there is another good reason that I keep contemplating flies, digging deep in the toilet and the whole of natural history. An obsessive reason, a fly in its own right whose buzzing I manage to drown out for a few hours while I study the rest of its species. Yet this fly stays inside me. The fly in my head needs a way out.

31

The fishing net is used to catch fish. Let us take the fish and forget the net. The snare is used to catch hares. Let us take the hare and forget the snare. The word is used to convey ideas. When ideas are understood, we can forget the words. How delightful to be able to talk with such a man, who has forgotten the words!

Chuang Tzu, Third Century B.C.

32

He collects stories,
But he himself doesn't have a story.

I get up late. Get dressed and go to the market. I rarely buy anything. I slowly wander around the stalls, looking at fruits and vegetables. I don't pay attention to the vendors. Just watching. Meditating on warm colors and round shapes. I call this exercise 'vitamins for the eyes.' Quite helpful when you are weary from gazing at letters all night long. Then I buy a newspaper. It doesn't matter which one. The newspaper and the cigarettes are an excuse to sit on a bench for more than an hour. It doesn't look strange. You read and you listen to people talking. Otherwise I'll forget how to talk. I don't feel like talking, I don't remember having spoken in the last few days, but I'm a good listener. In the café by the market, conversational themes change with the seasons. In May people talk of prom nights; in June—of forthcoming vacations; in July—of university exams; in August—of spoiled vacations; in September—of pickles and first-grade notebooks. All this is quite soothing. It means that somewhere, quite close to me actually, life is still peaceful and orderly like the lines of food in a smorgasbord. Sitting behind my newspaper, I hear people talk and I dissolve into their words like a sugar cube in a cup of coffee. If voyeurism is related to the eye and the gaze, what shall we call eavesdropping? Some sort of voyeurism for the ear.

Take these two thirtyish women sitting at my table and chatting. One is accompanied by her six-year-old (I'm guessing) son who is running around; each time he comes near his mother, the conversation stops for a moment while the boy gets his next piece of the cake, and then resumes as quickly as if it hasn't stopped at all. I'm almost invisible to them. At least they don't show any embarrassment. The childless one is the one who does the talking.

'It's been six years since we got married, and this idiot will never forgive me.'

'Jerk,' replies the other one.

'He only sleeps with me when I have my period. Five days a month. The rest of the time he won't even look at me. The more I fawn over him, the angrier he gets. Now that we're alone in our apartment, we could do it every day. Yes, but no. He yells at me, says he can't stand me: bitch, he says, you fucked the whole neighborhood before you married me.'

'What did he expect, for Christ's sake?'

'You couldn't wait for just one year, he says. Says I had promised him a virgin marriage, right out of a romance novel or something. Who does he think I am, Brooke Shields?'

'And you think Brooke Shields is a virgin! And then?'

'I should tell you I almost kept that promise. But he had to stay in Komi for two more months. After all, I'm not made of stone!' (Here I can't refrain from glancing at her over my coffee. She certainly isn't made of stone!—small, almost girlish, perky breasts, slightly expanding hips and toned, seductive legs with sun-kissed, almost invisible hair.) 'It just happened. You know how it is, you have a drink or two to unwind, and you think a groping hand is just a groping hand. I was twenty-five. The guy was stunned to see me bleeding. I must have been the last virgin in the neighborhood. Such a mess, I wished I could have died. And that was that, I never saw him again. He probably still curses the day he met me. Two weeks later Kapcho came back; we had already set the date for the wedding. Came loaded down with dinner sets and jewelry.'

'Gold is cheap over there in Komi.'

'He had made a nice pile of money and we had a great wedding. But when he saw I wasn't a virgin . . . he yelled that I had betrayed him, that he'd never as much as looked at a woman there, that he worked double shifts, the others were right to tease him for trusting me and working his ass off for me, while I was screwing around. He didn't touch me for three months. Then he waited for my period and that was the first time we ever had sex. I couldn't be your first, he said, but now every time will be like the first time. He didn't get off me for the five days when I was bleeding. I always have terrible cramps with my period, so I cried and screamed, but the more I tried to pull away from him, the better he felt. Like I was losing my virginity all over again.'

'Sick bastard. It's your fault for putting up with him.'

'He's got his own problems. He's not a bad person. If only it weren't for that . . . I don't know what he does the rest of the month. Jerking-off in the bathroom or fucking someone, I don't know. I begged him to do it just once when I don't have my period. If only I could get pregnant . . .'

I start feeling awkward. I get up and leave. Noticing me for the first time, they shut up and start sipping their coffees. On my way home I think about how for half an hour I've been closer to these women than their own husbands will ever be. What a sad ending. Somewhere there must be other men more intimate with your wife than you are.

33

Three of us are living here,
Playing chess and Black Maria . . .

OK, let's try again.

I was still living with Emma, but I had made a final decision to leave. Actually I made several final decisions to that effect but I kept putting it off. That's why this time I ordered a small truck for the following Saturday and I called three of my friends. I didn't have much luggage. The last night with Emma. We're sitting at the kitchen table, surrounded by boxes of books, two bags of clothes and my suit on a hanger, Jesus, my toxic-green wedding suit. I've taken the two cats in my lap and I'm stroking them. They always get restless when there's luggage in the room. They don't like being alone. I'll visit them sometime, I say. Bad move, Emma starts crying. I try to calm her. I really want to hug her but I know that if I do, I won't go and the agony will continue. We smoke in silence. We talk about trivial things. Despite everything I wanted this night to last longer. We had never been so close together. Somewhere there was a man I didn't know, in her there was a child who wasn't mine, and behind us—a couple of years with few peaceful days. I was wondering which one split us apart. During that night, however, neither seemed to exist. I wished something could happen to change things. At that very moment. At least some kind of sign. Our attachment to people is never as strong as when we're losing them.

'It's kicking,' Emma says, pointing to her belly. This must be the sign.

My wife's child. An example of a grammatically correct and still deeply mistaken phrase. There is a child between me and my wife. And this child's kicking against me. Taking strange steps in her womb. Starting from some obscure place to this room. Will he ever know that we have walked a couple of months together? That the door he opened had slammed behind me?

My grandmother used to say that if somebody must be born, somebody else has to die to make room for him. That evening we went to bed together for the first time in six months. I feigned sleep while Emma was hugging me. The cats also snuggled with us. What a sweet family. If only the child in Emma was not kicking so often. It was feeling cramped.

In the morning the truck came.

34

Matthew, Mark, Luke, John, where are you?
I can already walk on water . . .

Somewhere there lived an old man who was responsible for balance in the world. Not that anyone had called upon him to do so. The man just felt responsible for it. His usual occupation was gardening. He didn't talk to anyone. Many years ago he came to the village and bought a house at the edge of the village. They said he didn't pay very much because it had been empty for years and people swore they had seen strange fires in its windows at night. When the gardener moved in, everyone noticed the huge truck that brought him, filled with bundled books, crates of seeds and a big rocking chair, old and rotten, tied with wire at places. Ah, yes, and a cat. At the sight of these outlandish accessories the man was instantly recognized as crazy. That is, not one of the ordinary loonies the village was long used to, but one of those intellectuals who had gone nuts from too much reading. Had the village heard of Don Quixote, it would have been more precise with its diagnosis, but 'crazy' did just fine for the time being.

The old man was actually doing nothing wrong. Sometimes he didn't leave the house for days; he didn't even have a lamp on at night. It looked as though he'd gone somewhere.

Or he'd spend all his time in the garden, planting new seeds and grafting the plants. Sometimes he took the big chair out and sat in it, stroking the cat and staring at a tree. Strange, outlandish trees grew in his garden. Trees with big flat leaves, low bushes with tiny vermilion fruits, blue-chaliced tulips, huge prickly (beardy, as the villagers called them) trunks whose tops seemed as though they were on fire once a year in sumptuous flowers. Old wives swore that the garden was bewitched. A neighbor's pig once ventured into the garden and swelled up and died three hours later. The bees swarmed like mad at the garden with the weird blossoms and came back to their hives heavy and drunk.

Once a month the man went to the village post office and invariably sent one letter and one telegram. The addresses were always the same. The telegram—to some place in Sofia. And the letter . . . the address was written in a foreign language that the clerk could never decipher to the great disappointment of the whole village. When she copied stroke by stroke every letter on the envelope and sent it to her daughter in town, the village gasped at the name of the addressee. The addressee was the UN, the headquarters in New York. And while the telegram always contained the same text that the clerk was 'professionally obliged' to read in order to count the signs, no one knew what was in the letters to this over-important recipient. The telegrams consisted of the following two short sentences: 'I'm really OK now. I'm waiting for you.' The names of the addressees alternated. Two women with the same family name.

The last time the old man came to the post office he didn't look good. His eyes had sunken deeply in their sockets and his hand was shaking violently while he wrote the telegram. The clerk didn't even read the text, she already knew the number of signs by heart. This time, however, she noticed that there were only two words on the form. Words to make your flesh creep: I'm dead. The clerk objected that it was forbidden to write such things in a telegram. The man said nothing, just tore up the form, took a new one and wrote: I'm off. Paid and left. Two days later two women came to the village, most probably mother and daughter. They were dressed in black and this color looked especially becoming on the younger one. They got off the bus, they asked about such and such a man and they headed straight for the house of the mad gardener. Less then an hour later they came out and went to the town hall. They had a couple of talks and came back accompanied by two village men with shovels. The mayor gave them permission to bury the gardener in his own garden, behind the house. Something unheard of in this village. They buried him the same day and the two women caught the last bus back. The only thing they took from the house was an old leather-bound notebook. With time the whole garden grew rank and almost blocked the house from view. It still had that strange exotic look, the big-leafed tree grew enormous but nobody dared pass the gate.

For some time after the gardener's death, woeful feline wails wafted from the house but soon they too died away.

The notebook was old and bound by hand. Pocket-size, with a wire spiral. The leather, once cherry-colored, was now dark. The beautifully handwritten letters on the cover were still visible: *Notes of the Naturalist.*

35

Notes of the Naturalist

I'm starting over. I'm not sure that the letters I'm sending to the Organization reach their destination. I suppose they get plenty of letters over there. Yet someone must be reading them. Someone must come across one of mine. Because time goes by and things get worse. They get out of control. I'm doing what I can about the equilibrium but they have to be warned. I cannot hold out much longer on my own. I'm wondering if I made a mistake with the Organization. I have no other choice.

The house I have rented is a good one. It has a big, south-facing garden. The climate is also good; the winds are mild and low. The cat got used to it quickly, which shows that the place is really nice. Tomorrow I'll start cultivating the garden.

I'm trying to explain to the Organization that balance is at stake. And what's going to happen is not what everybody fears. The apocalypse is not that scary. The way they describe it, it's more of an illumination. World war is harmless. The apocalypse and war only serve to distract our attention. That's what they were sent for. What can happen any moment now is much deadlier and, alas, much harder to notice. It affects the hidden mechanisms of Earth and the universe. It won't be long before strange things start happening with us. Or they might already have started. Things that won't be as fiery as the apocalypse and therefore nobody will notice them at first. The worst is I cannot describe them in accurate detail. I have the words at hand but I can't do it. I mustn't. I suspect that a detailed and accurate description of what's coming will set its mechanism in motion. A detailed and accurate description will be the detonator; it will supply the formula for how things will develop. This makes my task incredibly hard. I must use another language. I'm trying gardening. Say it with plants, use their silent language that speaks with nothing but forms. I expect serious admonitions on their part. In my letters to the Organization I try to talk in allegories. I'm trying not to give too accurate a description of what's coming in order to avoid bringing together the words that might open the floodgates. But they obviously don't take my letters seriously. They don't comprehend the allegory.

It occurs to me that one of those six days of the Lord must have lasted a million of what we now call years. Thus I can reconcile God with Darwin. What the latter ascribes to millenary evolution and what the former created in mere days could be one and the same, if only I equalize the units of measure. One more thing: I suspect that there is someone in this world doing just the opposite of what I'm doing to keep the balance. The strangest thing is that he exists due to the same principle of natural equilibrium. Behind Darwin's back,

I could call him the Anti-Christ; behind God's back (which is much harder) I could call him anti-evolutionist. I can see him peeling words off things, the way you peel an apple.

The imbalances stalking us show up everywhere, but I think the most horrible one is the imbalance between the names of things and the things themselves. Things have started slipping out of their names like peas from a dry pod. So far names had clung close to things in an inseparable whole, just as the atoms of hydrogen and oxygen formed the molecule of water. And when man managed to separate the hydrogen atoms from the oxygen atoms, incredible energy was released. Imagine that energy multiplied a million times and you'll get an idea what will befall us when names are finally separated from things. I think there will be no explosion, but rather something much more horrid. I will not give it a name for the time being. Because the names create the named.

We must talk only in allegories.

There are invisible scales. For greater clarity we could picture them like ordinary open-market scales. The weights are always on one side. No matter whether we measure beans, or mackerel, or plain crab apples, we look at the weights and we say: here's a pound of beans, or mackerel, or crab apples, etc. We say so when the scales are balanced and one pan holds the words, the other—things. But what will happen if the words swarm and shove the things, and then leave them like the queen bee leaves the hive with her swarm? They will start playing with themselves, measuring each other. Weights in one scale, weights on the other, i.e., measures, words, call them as you wish. And both scale pans will shout: we are mackerel, we are crab apples, we are black beans. And nobody will ever be able to set them straight or even tell them apart.

Did the guys in the Organization understand my story about the weights? I will keep writing though. I must find out where words breed. I must reach their nest, their litter, their hatch. I don't know what to call it. And I must avoid accurate names. I've been looking for that place for many years. So many I haven't even counted them. What did I do before that? I don't remember anything, I don't wish to remember. I must find out how words breed. I'm watching the plants in my garden. I've bought a pile of botanical manuals.

These chives here and that bulbous meadow-grass (*Poa Vivitara*) over there reproduce by parthenogenesis, i.e., agamically. The new plants are born from tubers, bulbs derived from their parents, and they have the same hereditary qualities as their parents do. Reproduction through the root system. Could words have resorted to this simplest method of reproduction? I don't believe they blundered so. With this method of reproduction, new words would be indistinguishable from the old ones. And still there must be something to it, since both words and plants have roots. There must be something. Books quote the early depletion of the genetic fund as the main evolutionary disadvantage of this method. Pollination offers a much greater variety. Wind or bees, wasps, chafers and all kinds of insects could carry the pollen for dozens, for hundreds of miles. If the pollen of this birch over there rise with the air currents at about a mile and a half, which is perfectly possible, they will travel five hundred miles from here. And words are so much lighter than pollen. Why has nobody ever calculated the weight of a word? Just approximately. I suppose different words weigh differently. Damn it, I hate such negligence. They know the weight of the pollen seed, a mere speck of dust, while nobody cared to measure the word. Does it assume the weight of the voice pronouncing it or the weight of the ink in which it was written? I cannot find any Natural History of Words. Not anywhere.

Here are some questions whose answers I have not yet found:

Do words have sexes?

Is sex the same as gender?

If a word is of the masculine gender, shall we consider it male?

If words come in both sexes, when and how does intercourse take place?

Do letters carry their sexual characteristics?

If so, how is the alphabet divided sexually?

Can we accept that vowels are female and consonants are male, or is the division more complicated than that?

Could words be basically sexless but acquire the sex of the man or woman mouthing them?

If so, what happens when male words enter a female mouth?

What happens when the word is merely written? What sex would it be?

I feel a growing suspicion that the whole mess started with writing. How many devils sit on top of a letter . . . There is something Satanic in words which have outlived their authors. I don't know why others don't feel it, but for me this is vintage vampirism. There is a dead man laid out in every written word. I shudder as I write this. Because I, too, have built myself a nice coffin with this notebook. I hope I find the strength to burn it before I die. I don't want to become undead in these written pages. Though now that I think of it, aren't spoken words the same? As we speak, we—by the way—slyly plant those seeds in the heads of other people. Like pollen. Radio can take them much farther than air currents. Yes, the only pure use of words is thought. Words should be thought. Nothing but. At least for a year. I have to warn the Organization. I know it's cruel but it's the only way. Things have gone too far. Indiscriminate procreation of names. They already carry the taint. We don't know how to disinfect them. A horrible infection is coming, more horrible than AIDS. Dead men's words. Words that curdle human relationships as illness can curdle a new mother's milk.

I realize that what I wrote the other night was obscure and complicated. But that's the only way I am allowed to express myself. Otherwise I'd be helping Evil. But I won't supply the formula. I'll take it away with me. Here I must mention my father, may he rest in peace, who first started the struggle for equilibrium. My mother said he was nuts, left him and ran away with another man. I stayed with him and helped him. He didn't write a single line. The times he said something unrelated to his preoccupations can be counted on the fingers of one hand. I have inherited his dislike for idle talk—my mother used to call it surliness. My father was a self-educated naturalist, a naturalist-naivist. He loved to muse on the names of the flowers. Made out the Latin names without ever having studied Latin, relating them to names he knew. Sometimes he grumbled, apparently finding disparity between the flower and its name. He regularly consulted a gardening manual, the same one I'm using. One of those books which inform you that the lotus was the favorite flower of the ancient Egyptians and the tulip came from Asia. In fact these were precisely the facts he was interested in. 'The leek appears in the national emblem of Wales,' my father would read and Wales would seem to grow in his garden. And when he put some leeks on the table, they were no mere leeks but symbols, heraldry. The bitter fibrous husks held stories, History itself was sleeping there. Nothing was merely what it seemed. And so he maintained balance in the world through his relationships with leeks. My father knew that anybody who doesn't honor the leeks on his table is offending the honor of Wales. Wales would have a reason for—justified—protest, and a conflict would ensue. That's why my father always said a benediction to Wales when a stalk of leek happened to grace his table. With great tact and diplomacy he begged forgiveness for those who in their ignorance and thoughtlessness did not even know what they were chewing. This was his mission. And thus, while he was alive, he managed to keep the fragile equilibrium in the world.

Sometimes books play weird jokes on us. Years ago I worked hard on one of my ideas. I thought this would be my legacy, something beautiful and to some extent practical. I knew that different flowers opened up at different times of the day. I spent two years searching botanical books and meadows; I roamed the fields for days on end. I wanted to find the appropriate flowers and, planting them in a circle, to create a natural clock. A clock with a natural mechanism. Asked what the time was, people would no longer answer '3 P.M.' but 'tulip.' I was proud of my idea. And then, two days before the planting of the flowers I had already collected, I happened, just happened to read in the trivia section of a newspaper the following note: 'Carl Linnaeus, the father of botany, knowing the precision of botanical cycles, planted in the sections of a circle flowers that opened up at specific times of the day.' Why did I never come across this information when I searched all sorts of reference books? Words had tricked me once again. While I was gathering flowers, happy to be doing something yet unknown, they snickered at me and carefully selected the moment for their appearance. Once again I was convinced that we don't really control texts; they dance around us. They hide somewhere while we are looking for them, and they alone pick the time to appear before us. Something must be done.

For the last few months I'm trying to do what I never dared to. I don't have the time to wait for plant instructions. It's time for radical action. Time to enter the beehive. The maximum concentration of words, the swarm of words. I don't know what's the acceptable way to say it, in short—I'm going inside the text. Yes, I break into books. I hope my ex-wife and her charming daughter will never come across these notes, because they will be the final proof of my diagnosis. Yet I have no other choice. I have discovered that books—and not all books, but just novels, and not all novels, but just a few select ones (I own them, but I'll never give away their names) contain the queen words who are ready to fly out and swarm the unnamable. How could I keep these books with the others, let them rest their infected covers on the covers of innocent books! They must be kept locked away in a palm-tree chest, because the palm-tree is beatific and can isolate the evil. The palm-tree chest must then be locked inside a chest of iron, and the chest of iron must be buried deep in clay soil so that nothing will sprout on it. Those books must never ever be burned: first, because it is a sin to burn a book, and second, because the fire could just release their dark energy. And these books are dangerous just because they describe what I'm unwilling to name in accurate and great detail. Once upon a very old time one of those books had broken into my life and was wrecking it daily. When things tumbled down and, despite our happy marriage, my wife got suddenly pregnant by another man (we were keeping a period of continence), I started sinking into those peculiar states that still continue to plague me, on and off . . . And then, just then I had the strange feeling that I've already read that somewhere. What was happening to me was coming right out of some bad novel, a novel I had read. I rummaged through my library, I rummaged my friends' libraries and I found it. Everything coincided, page by page, sentence by sentence, word by word. My own private apocalypse.

In the last few days I've been carefully studying the novels

I set apart as particularly dangerous. I'm taking my time. I must come well prepared, as the beekeeper opens the hive unnoticed by the bees. The trick is to suppress your fear because they can smell it. Stop perspiring. Fear settles in your perspiration, that's why it smells so bad. You must have no smell, you must move smoothly so they can accept you as one of their own, as a big and rather slow bee. It's the same with novels. Harder actually, because my body is superfluous. I must leave it and—naked as a word—wedge my way among them. A word among words.

I'm feeling more and more prepared. I'm looking for cracks in the text where I could creep through. I think it would be unwise to enter through the beginning. Novels start strong, in the beginning the syntax is tense and I would be easy to spot. I need some lyrical digression, some detailed description to distract the words so that I could slip in like a leaf shaken by a sudden wind, or like a lizard slinking under a stone.

I've got a few personal matters to take care of. Tomorrow I will post my last telegram. I don't want my body to stay discarded. I believe they will come this time. I've left a letter asking them to bury me under the palm tree in the garden. I'm concerned about the cat though, poor creature, I wonder how she'll handle it. I can only hope that someday we will meet again in another novel. This is about all. Taking leave took less time than I expected. My mission continues. In fact it just started. Well, I'm off.

36

*3 big oranges, a cup of sugar, some cornmeal,
10 cherries, some ginger . . .*

A recipe for orange soup

Saturday. Drizzling rain, cold and damp. A perfect day for banana fish. A perfect day for Salinger, in fact. You relax because nothing worse can happen to you.

No author is better suited for such weather, although Salinger is like an umbrella to soak under. Even Eliot is jollier. Perfect for some dry October day.

This is what crosses my mind while I'm taking Salinger out in the train compartment. I'm not the talkative type and I see books as my shield against those endless conversations that always start with destination inquiries and flow over to kids and kidney problems. Besides, I don't have an acceptable answer for the point, the end point of my journey. I had bought a ticket to the last station but I could just as well get off at the next stop.

I love this book because it's so unassuming, at least on the outside. A simple cover without illustrations. I'm sure that the name of the author doesn't mean anything to the travelers on this train, which reduces my chances of being talked to. I was early and the other passengers are only now starting to fill the train. I can't read before we've departed so I look at the corridor. I'm trying to guess which passenger will enter my compartment. I'm rarely lucky enough to have a beautiful woman to look at. There's only one place left and I have almost lost hope. The train is already departing when she comes. At first I pay no notice, merely registering her entrance—thirtyish, no luggage, sitting across from me by the window. The usual conversations start, but are rather brief. The woman and I seem to be the only ones not taking part in them; I am absorbed in my book and she is looking out of the window. This time, though, I'm finding it hard to read. I look at her a few times, or rather at her reflection in the windowpane. Without being particularly beautiful, she is totally out of place in this situation—the compartment with its nondescript passengers and dirty curtains, the train, the lousy weather. I feel a strong desire to start talking to her, to go smoking with her in the corridor. I've never known how these things work. With grace and levity, I suppose, though I have neither. A newly divorced man who thinks of nothing but his ex-wife. Almost dramatically, I take my pack out and leave the compartment. I slowly chain-smoke two cigarettes but the woman doesn't stir. On entering the compartment I see her noting something down on a folded sheet of paper. I, too, like to jot down certain things on the train, but I always do it secretly, shying away from the stares of my fellow travelers. This woman, however, is unperturbed. She takes long pauses, looks out of the window, then adds another word. I imagine charming her with Salinger. I naturally lack the courage to talk to her. All the lines that come to me sound stupid and blandly transparent. I close the book over my forefinger to give her a better view of the title. For all I know, this might mysteriously unleash something, result in something. A special woman would appreciate this title. A pretty mouth, and her eyes—as far as I can see in the dwindling light—are green. No reaction. At each station I shudder and pray she doesn't get off the train.

I try a vile technique of slander and abasement. The sour grapes technique. I imagine her in tattered stockings, with rotting teeth, seated on a toilet. Then my imagination soars. I make up a whole history for her—married with two, no, three children (so her breasts would be sagging more), a teacher of literature wasting her bespectacled evenings over a pile of notebooks while her boring husband is drinking a lot in front of the TV . . . I have mastered this technique to perfection and I can swear it works almost every time. This woman, though, seemed to come away unscathed; what's more, she turned my technique against me. The situations I concocted chipped nothing away from her image. On the contrary, they reinforced it and kindled my desire. I imagined us discussing the ending of 'Teddy' in bed. I take the view that Salinger was faking it here: the ending is too transparent and predictable for more than a page. Too bad. That could be her line.

As I was arranging the scene, I barely managed to see her leaving the compartment. The train had stopped. She was getting off. I had no time to lose. I grabbed my bag and I got off at the same station. I nearly bumped into her. She looked at me for the first time; her eyes weren't green. I apologized and I blurted the first thing that came to mind, just to stop her from going away: A perfect day for banana fish, isn't it? Then two, no, three kids ran to her and each one wanted to hug her.

The train had gone. I slowly took my bag and went searching for a hotel. I'd forgotten to check the name of the town at the station and when I asked the receptionist, she gave me a horrified look. She did give me a key, however. Room 507. The number sounded familiar. I went in, turned the key and took the book out of my bag. Everything happens for a reason, I thought. The book opened at page 26, on the left. I read the final paragraph eleven times:

He got off at the fifth floor, walked down the hall, and let himself into 507. The room smelled of new calfskin luggage and nail-lacquer remover.

He glanced at the girl lying asleep on one of the twin beds. Then he went over to one of the pieces of luggage, opened it, and from under a pile of shorts and undershirts he took out an Ortgies calibre 7.65 automatic. He released the magazine, looked at it, then reinserted it. He cocked the piece. Then he went over and sat down on the unoccupied twin bed, looked at the girl, aimed the pistol, and fired a bullet through his right temple.

Then I must have fallen asleep.

37

I suppose Man was made oblivious of his own beginnings. We cannot recollect our birth. Memory does not function yet, that center in our brain isn't ready. The beginning is shapeless and obscure. The sum of several accidents setting in motion a series of inevitable events. And still the door to the beginning is never fully closed. There is always a crack—small enough to stop us from entering and big enough to ooze soft, rosy, seductive light.

We will never be loved as much as we were when we were children. That is why childhood is such a cruel time. Its cruelty is in what will come later. Where does this love go after that? Why do we spend the rest of our lives wanting to be loved as we once were? for no other reason than that we exist? For the last few days I've lived in my childhood more often and for longer periods of time. I experience everything so vividly—eidetic behavior, my psychiatrist says—that sometimes I come back with my knees bruised and, once, with a bump on my head. I don't share this with my psychiatrist, there's no point. When I'm back in my childhood I mostly find myself in a cherry tree. I'm not doing anything special, nothing but sitting on a branch, eating cherries and spitting out the pits. Buddha sat under a tree for seven years. What kind of tree was it? Never mind. I'm sitting in the cherry tree for seven years (the first seven) watching white turn green and green turn red. Seven times. Seven slow years of white, green and red. The cherry, the cherry will be the tree of the Bulgarian Buddha. Yet Bulgaria is not the point here. Children have no fatherland. Their fatherland is childhood. To make up for it, they have fathers. Well, so to speak. Their fathers go to work, they aren't there. Can a father be a nine-to-five cashier or vice-president or clerk or hustler, then come back home and be a father for a few hours? You caaaan't, I mumble from the cherry tree, my mouth full of pits like a Demostenes practicing oration with pebbles under his tongue. OK, I'll spit it out: we can only have epiphanies in our childhood, in those seven years when we are left to our own devices. Seven years outside society. Seven years of statelessness. Seven years of anarchy. Every day is fully yours. Every day serves no other purpose but to make the world your playground. See those ants, what a cherry, and that fly over there, what if I catch it, what if I tear one wing away, look how it spins around the table, what if I tear both . . . !

Last night I dreamed of the phrase 'my childhood wife.' This morning I recalled all the wives I had in my childhood, with my mother naturally topping the list.

At least a dozen wives and not a single divorce. No pain at all.

38

Where does all this excess love go,
Who's the sweeper, who throws away the trash,
Where is the garbage can?

When the marriage is over and the last dinner set has already been divided, there's one more thing to divide: friends. Every family creates an environment, a biocenosis populated by relatives, family friends and the odd acquaintance. Emma and I had too many guests. She was good at entertaining. I was a different case. When I'd had enough, I locked myself in the bathroom. Everybody knew what this meant and filed away with no hard feelings, saying goodbye through the door. When Emma and I divorced, at first nobody believed it. We had been the perfect family. They were shocked, not knowing how to react. The occasional attempts to meet me separately (and, I suppose, Emma) were tragic. The absence of the other was palpable. As one of them put it, it was like three persons getting together for a game of bridge, dealing out the cards and pretending there's nothing wrong. He was right. Most of them avoided mentioning Emma in my presence and that only made things worse. I wanted to talk about her.

Strange how people think that the aftermath of a divorce is like the aftermath of a catastrophe: nothing is the same. The world was supposed to be split in two and Emma and

I were supposed to be living in its opposite halves. And yet the world had stayed together. We lived in the same city and, as I had rented an apartment in the same neighborhood, we used the same buses and shopped at the same places. One grocer kept asking me why I was buying a loaf of bread when my wife had already bought one. A couple of times I passed by the windows of her apartment. It was late, the curtains were drawn, the light was on. Once I saw one of the cats on the windowsill, between the curtain and the pane. Did she see me, too? I knew I shouldn't go there. Emma was already living with the other guy, I don't know what to call him, OK, with the father.

39

I will be an ice-cream vendor,
Going broke in winter's splendor.

Today I have to fix the rocking chair. It almost disintegrated while I was moving out of the house. I found some fine wire. I ought to find a job, too. I had a look at the market. I could be selling something seasonal. Or, at best, newspapers in a kiosk. I've always wanted a job like that. I could read all the newspapers or even write. These days I'm rarely up to it. I sit down and have a cigarette but it just won't work. My friend the psychiatrist was quick to give the diagnosis: an inability to concentrate, obsessiveness and anancasm, if I remember correctly. It's true that my notes have grown short and chaotic. I started with the idea of a novel. Well, it's going to be a fragmented one.

Anancasm (Gr, ananke—obsession): a condition whereby the sufferer cannot stop recounting certain experiences despite realizing their futility and abnormality. Such experiences could be ideas, desires, fears or impulses. They haunt the sufferer incessantly, usually in the same manner. A. is a psychoneurotic syndrome. Psychoanalysis sees A. as based on a relevant ego-impairing inner conflict. Usually manifested in persons with prior insecurities caused by an improper processing of early childhood experiences. These persons could be inclined to manage fear through a 'counter-magic.'

Dictionary of Psychology

Sometimes I feel a strange desire to walk the streets at dusk and look into the ground-floor windows. Kitchen windows, where normal families can be seen. What kind of domestic voyeurism is this?

. . . and a string of weasel testicles protects women against unwanted pregnancies.

An old Irish remedy

If you want to write a Natural Novel, you must watch the visible world closely. You must find resemblances. Each autumn the cabbages mock the raised-collar style from the time of Marie Antoinette. Or Marie Antoinette had an eye for cabbages. Who can say whether history is influenced by botany or vice versa? The Novel of Natural History makes no such distinctions. Yesterday the market was full of decapitated Antoinettes.

. . . now she is the mother of her child the mother of her child repeat it slowly I must get used to it she's not a woman anymore she is a mother something else a pine-cone maybe and a bee a mother—honeycomb—her child's hive . . .

Once I came home later than usual. Emma was talking on the kitchen phone and didn't hear me. I, however, heard the following phrase: 'A drone, he's just a drone, although he's not a bad man.' I was struck by the fact that this phrase was the exact replica of something her father had said years ago and I had once again overheard.

Why do I keep replaying that phrase in my head? What does it matter a few months after the divorce? People sometimes say such things without meaning to.

A drone, he's just a drone, although he's not a bad man.

Drones are born from unfertilized eggs; therefore they have no fathers. They have the genetic characteristics of their mother and of the drone that fertilized their grandmother.

I tell myself this is important and continue leafing through the several beekeeping guides in my possession. I will never be free from that phrase until I stuff it with information. Until it swells like a tick and releases its grip on me.

The drone has a large body—15 to 17 mm long. It has well-built chest muscles and wings which allow it to fly at a great speed and distance. In the lower part of its back there are sophisticated and well-developed reproductive organs.

So far Emma had said nothing bad about me.

The purpose of drones is to fertilize the bees in their wedding flights. If they come across other hives, the bees are glad to accept them.

Not bad, not bad at all.

. . . but in the second half of summer, when the main melliferous flowers have withered and the incoming nectar is sparse, the swarming instinct disappears and drones become superfluous. The bees isolate them from the honey and, starving them, expel them through the entrance of the hive.

The entrance of the hive becomes a natural exit for the drones, *exitus letalis*.

What does the structure of bee families tell us, what kind of analogies does it offer? I suspect that God created this rather peculiar family to tell us something. I can't exactly pin it down, but it is a clue. Yesterday I read in the newspaper that the fin-de-millennium tendency pushed men further and further away from the family. Women preferred raising their children alone and the future belonged to families of two (excluding the father).

A drone, he's just a drone, although he's not a bad man.

40

Somewhere people live in houses with an 'a' . . .

Many years ago, when I was a small boy, I used to live in the country. The world looked gorgeous, as if just washed by rain. After everything that happened between me and Emma I decided to go back there for a while. To substitute my recent memories for those distant days and nights of my childhood. Emma didn't belong there so I hoped she would leave me alone. I didn't last a week. Nothing was the same, nothing. That village was gone. The spell was broken. The eccentric people whose stories I used to enjoy now just seemed grim and depressing. Slowly but surely the village was going insane. I saw madness everywhere. Half the old men were fighting for the best graveyard lots. The graveyard was full, but everybody wanted to be buried at a better spot, somewhere closer to their relatives. 'I don't want nothing else,' my grandmother wailed, 'just to be buried closer to my little Kale. I want to talk to her, tuck her in at night, cuddle her . . .' Little Kale was her first daughter, died at the age of three, and my grandmother never got over her.

Grandpa said she almost lost her mind. She'd made a doll the size of a child (a scarecrow, Grandpa said); she carried it everywhere, talked to it, tried to feed it and took it to bed at night. One night Grandpa burnt the doll. He was a soft-hearted man so I can imagine how much it must have hurt him. Yet Grandma was saved.

Mad Risto, the last person in the village to wear a sheep-skin hat in summer (a detonated shell from the last war made him insensible to temperature), sits every morning at the village square right below the simple monument of the victims of that same war. Poking at the dirt, he asks passersby the time, then says, like he has for fifty-three years: 'What a day, blink and it's over.'

Tin Dikko is one of those who went nuts from too much reading. His cabin is made of empty cheese boxes. His pet rabbit lives in a crate on the roof. Dikko's got his own borehole of a well and he takes the water out in an empty lemonade bottle tied on a string. He's grown a long unkempt beard like Robinson Crusoe. That's what the village people call him. The man was 'slightly unhinged,' in my grandma's euphemistic, Christian phrasing.

Once upon a time I had found the stories of Mad Risto and Tin Dikko amusing. Now these people—they are still alive—fill me with gloom.

A dying village that's still trying to tell you its increasingly mirthless, lifeless stories. I heard that people had started paying Devil Dinyo, the semi-blind caretaker of the village church, to ring the bells for them: 'Ring them so we can hear them while we're still alive, because when we die and scare away the crows, God knows what we will hear.'

Death was the only adventure they prepared themselves for. Some old men had ordered cheap tombstones and they kept them at home with the name, year of birth and the first three figures of the year of death already chiseled. The only gravedigger left in the village was treated to endless glasses of brandy for the promise to dig you the best grave ever. Everybody imagined they would die in winter. As one of them said, summer was no time for dying, what with all that work to do, hay to store and vines to harvest . . .

Once, when the village was big and lively, the district authorities wanted to make it a town. This was considered prestigious, but the local folks gave it some thought and said no. The only reason they gave was that towns had policemen, policemen who would piss on their hedgerows and stare at their wives. Those people just watched out for their wives and hedgerows, that's all.

And I turned out to be a poor watchman. I wouldn't even dare burn a sacrificial doll.

41

*I don't trust anything that bleeds every month
and doesn't die.*

Men's room graffiti

. . . and she found out where the other one lived, got there,
grabbed her and dragged her home to her husband: and now
to bed, she said, since you want each other so much, right here
before me . . . they tried to resist but she was screaming and
pounding so badly that they lay down, now get started or else,
she shouted—and they did, what else could they do . . . while
she stood by the door and watched and watched and watched,
and then she said 'poor sweeties' and left.

. . . white chocolate, prime quality white chocolate. Every
time she was late she brought her husband a bar of white
chocolate. He craved the stuff so much he didn't see the
crumpled dress, he didn't smell the other man on her—nothing, nothing at all. He munched on the chocolate and said
nothing while she disappeared into the bathroom. Who
knows how she'd come up with the white chocolate, was
she joking or feeling guilty or remorseful or was she merely
trying to distract him? For one year it was bar after bar after
bar of white chocolate. The man was probably sick of it but
nevertheless ate it in silence. He said nothing and she thought

she'd got the knack of it. Then one night she came home to an empty house. She opened the closet—no shoes, no coat. A suitcase was missing, too. She checked the bathroom and there, on the mirror, he had written with her own lipstick: '186 chocolates!'

Stories I've overheard in the café by the market.

42

Linnaeus had a proverbial passion for classifications. Perhaps such was the passion of the whole eighteenth century. Having classified all known plants by genus and species and having given them their simple names (*nomina trivia*), he made another, less famous systematization: *floræ officiarii,* or 'the officers' flora,' ranking all his botanical friends and foes in a strict hierarchy. Services and friendships earned the botanists—or the natural historians, as most of them still called themselves—the rank of colonels, lieutenants, majors and so on, down to plain sergeant majors and corporals. This army was naturally led by General Linnaeus personally. One of his touchier contemporaries (probably a corporal) Lametrie wrote a caustic article under the beautiful title 'The Man-Plant,' where he inverted Linnaeus' method or just his analogies and classified human beings as homosporous, angiosperm and gymnosperm.

There is something in this Lametrie, a nice slip of our anthropocentrism. Why should Man be at the hub of all analogies? How would plants describe us, I wonder, what classification would they impose on us? 'Described by a

Plant' sounds like a good title to be used later. I feel we're being watched: by rubber plants, sparrow-grass, bonsai, small date palms, Chinese roses, geraniums and lemon trees. They keep an eye on us. Let me (as a good naturalist) add a private observation: as the scandals between me and my wife multiplied, the leaves of the rubber plant in the living room withered and fell.

43

Goats and roses were courting near me . . .

The plant and the fly, as well as all other living creatures, appeared in this world millions of years earlier than Man. Was God just preparing the cradle and nursery of Man? Wouldn't it be fairer—fairer on a universal scale—if God had made Man as the plaything of all preceding plants and animals, a velvety, walking doll they could take care of? Human thought is too egocentric to allow such a possibility. Yet we could allow for it, at least here, on paper, in a couple of lines. We are the perfect entertainment to the fly buzzing in the room and to the rubber plant in the corner by the window. We think we own them, but as a matter of fact they own us. They watch our pointless wandering around from the top of their own Olympus and when they get bored they send out imperceptible signals to guide us.

I know, I know that in the very beginning of the Book, in Genesis, God says:

'Be fruitful and multiply; fill the earth and subdue it. Have dominion over the fish of the sea, the birds of the air, the cattle and all the animals that crawl on the earth.' How our heart rejoices to hear about that 'dominion' . . .

Well yes, but this is from the human Bible. How would the issue be rendered in the Fly Bible or the Plant Bible? Flies and plants have more genesis under their belt. How does a Fly Bible sound? Quite respectable, I would think. And ancient. Let's read a few lines. Just the beginning. You know my weakness for flies and beginnings. Just a note before I start. The book of flies would certainly use no paper, it would be, how shall I put it, a book of air. So we start. The Bible of Flies.

It might be a bit unclear. I said I understand some of their language. I've been observing them. Now I will try to translate for you. Quite roughly of course. There's always something lost in translation. In this case the first casualties would be the flight and the three-dimensional vision. Still, it would go like this:

1:1 In the beginning [was] air. And [God] said: let there be movement. And [there was] movement.

1:2 Then [God] created the wings. The wings carried nothing, yet drifted through the void. And [God] said: Let there be a body to those wings. And [there was] a body. But the body saw nothing. And said [God]: Let there be eyes in that body. And [there were] eyes.

1:3 And everything else was yielded by the eye, and there was nothing that the eye did not yield. And the eye wished for light and [there was] light. It wished for heaven and earth and it saw heaven and earth. And then it wished for animate beasts and humans and feces and it saw animate beasts and humans and feces. And said [the eye]: Behold, this is good, and it flew down to them.

1:4 And so [God] created flies in His own image. And when He created them He blessed them: be fruitful and multiply, and replenish the earth, and subdue it; and have dominion over the fish of the sea and over the fowl of the air and over every living thing that moveth upon the earth.

I think that's it, if I have got it correctly. Some words are always lost and therefore I hint at them in brackets, mostly with 'God.' This word always sounds right. As you can see, the 1:4 text is the same as in the human Bible. I couldn't claim for certain who borrowed from whom. So much for the Bible of Flies. For plants, I admit, I can't say anything yet. I just suppose that their writing resembles forms of leaves, roots, petals and stigmas.

I know that in 1758 the ubiquitous 'general' Linnaeus wrote a study on *Somnus Plantaram*, but I haven't come across it yet. I envy him the title. The sleeping of plants. Just perfect for a *natural novel*.

44

'I think I discovered something important,' F. told me one day.

'Important?'

'I think it's important.'

'And when did you discover it?'

'Yesterday. Yesterday afternoon.'

'Don't you remember the exact hour?'

'I don't have a wristwatch. Well, I could look at the clock but . . . Is this important?'

'Enough of this *importance*. Of course it is important, your discovery must be recorded precisely.'

'I didn't know,' F. whispered.

'Who will believe a discovery made yesterday afternoon . . .'

'I didn't know,' F. repeated crestfallen. 'But I might recall it if I try.'

'. . . So?'

'It was at the time flies drift in reverie through the air, most of them napping on the curtain.'

'That's not precise enough.'

'I remember the sun was not very hot anymore.'

'Not enough.'

'The stylus of the gramophone. The sun was illuminating the stylus of the gramophone. This is important. And concrete.'

'OK, OK, we'll record it like that: A discovery made yesterday afternoon when flies drift in reverie through the air and the sun is shining on the gramophone stylus. Is that OK?'

'Sounds like a poem. And it's concrete,' F. said emphatically.

'I don't like poems. We must also record the name of the discoverer.'

'Must we?'

'You're killing me with this *must we*. It's your discovery, isn't it?'

'Well yes. Do you think anyone will be interested in the author?'

'I'm not really sure. The author has no status anymore.'

'I don't know what you're getting at.'

'He died.'

'Who did?'

'The author. In 1968. Have you never read Barthes?'

'Never.'

'How about Lyotard? *The Postmodern Explained to Children*?'

'I'm not a child.'

'It's not really for children.'

'I wouldn't touch a book that lies in its title.'

'OK then, what was the discovery?'

'Ah . . . damn . . . I think I forgot it.'

'You think you forgot it?'

'Don't be angry with me. It must not have been that important. Still, we had a great afternoon. An afternoon spent in pleasantly pointless conversations.'

I like my conversations with F. She always knows what I'm looking for. What's wrong in chatting with a fly? I'm alone and I can do whatever I want. She's my friend. And she's very nice. No, we don't have a sexual relationship. Anything else?

'You have recorded our pleasant pointless afternoon conversations?' F. is more scared than surprised.

'And I've prepared them for publication.'

'And you've prepared them for publication? Then they weren't pointless.'

'On the contrary, they were. At least such was my intention.'

'An intention for pointless conversations' . . . F. is being sarcastic.

'Why not? Nobody has published a book of pointless conversations. A book about trifles, about flies, about your own self.'

'You're nuts. You will be declared insane. A book of pointless conversations. Shared stories. With whom, if I may ask? With a fly? Do you really plan to publish this book?'

'Well . . . in fact I'm wondering if I can't make it a film script.'

'Wow . . . a movie!'

'Yes, maybe a movie is more like it. Nobody ever made a movie of trifles, of useless things. A movie made of what's normally left out of movies.'

'A movie made of trashed scraps of film?'

'Not quite. These things aren't even on the scraps.'

'I don't get it.'

'In this movie the protagonist will lie idly on the bed on Sunday afternoon. The protagonist just hangs around his apartment, goes to the toilet, looks through old newspapers there, flushes and yawns. He may not speak at all. And no inner voices. A man deep in his thoughts which remain unknown to us. Depressing thoughts, on the whole. Everyday thoughts.'

'A bit like *you*, yes?'

'And worse. A slo-o-o-ow movie, where even tragedies lack a climax. A movie with no society, no message. A movie about dead things.'

'I like that. Dead. Something like the flies of the 1960s. Nobody remembers them anymore.'

'The sixties were a great time.'

'Were they? You can't remember them.'

'So I have read. *Le grand refus*! The great refusal. Imagination was everything. The flower revolution. Important years.'

'Imporant people. They try to remember those years. But I don't like it when they try too hard.'

'They were all young in the sixties.'

'Everybody wants to make his youth sound terribly important.'

'Right, but . . .'

'But nobody remembers the flies of the sixties,' F. is shaking. 'Nobody remembers them. There were swarms of flies in 1968.'

'OK, so this is what my movie or my book, if I ever come to publish it, will be about. The big flies of the sixties that came to nothing. Nothing at all.'

45

Nothing, Nothing, Nothing, Nothing, Nothing, Nothing, Nothing, Nothing, Nothing. I have only a few pages left and I can fill them like that. What's behind those seven letters? Nothing. All the futility of life.

Today is the first anniversary of my divorce with Emma.

There are some dreams and other trifles I haven't collected yet.

Dreams are like cats, the last to leave their former homes.

Everybody's talking about the end. Like kids trying to scare each other. It's been the same game ever since Revelation. Blood and fire, a flood, a collision with a meteorite, an ecological catastrophe, an ozone hole and another dozen surefire prophecies.

For me there is something scarier than the end—the lack of an end. I'm horrified to think that an ending might be impossible. That is more of an apocalypse than all the other apocalypse stories put together. There is no ending.

After everything that happened in this year of my life, the Earth was supposed to crack, the skies should have fallen or at least the ozone hole should have grown significantly bigger. Nothing of the sort happened. I am still alive. The neighbors give me funny looks but I don't care about them. I can stop going out altogether. And I can take my pen and my chair and never come back. I have to look for an ending. How was it . . . to release that fly in my head. Just a little hole.

46

The sun is shining. It's a good day to take a walk. Fred is fishing. The rain is falling. The rose is beautiful. Grandma is knitting. The year has twelve months, every month has around thirty days, and every day has 24 hours. The cat is purring. I'm sitting on a chair. Autumn is coming. Winter has come. It started snowing. The trees are green in spring. It's summer.

Why isn't everything as simple as a first-grade primer?

47

This tramp is so drunk
That when he pees under the sky
The spurt alone keeps him from falling.
Male haiku

Today started much better. I felt like shaving. I even went to the market. Well, the world was not particularly moved by my absence. Same here. I bought a new notebook and two pencils. I can't use a pen, it's too definitive for me. I wonder why I'm feeling so good today. I'm not used to it. I bought the notebook because I intend to write a new novel. The idea sounds good to me: a tramp in a rocking chair. The image came first. The tramp, a regular hobo, stinking, unshaven, an old hat, is sitting in his rocking chair somewhere near the garbage dump. Dogs are peacefully sleeping around him. An emaciated cat is lounging in his lap. The chair is rocking gently, as if moved by the wind. It would look good on camera. The tramp in the rocking chair. Peaceful and even kind of aristocratic. All other sounds have been muffled except that gentle creak. This will be the leading episode, followed by the story of the tramp. It started as an experiment. The man wanted to write a novel with a tramp for a protagonist, yet he was so determined to make everything real that he decided to mingle with the hobos and try to live their life for a week. He chose a different neighborhood so he wouldn't be recognized. He grew a beard, tipped a shabby hat over his eyes and changed beyond recognition. The first two nights he came home to bathe and sleep, but then he decided that this would compromise the purity of his experiment, so he searched for another place to sleep. He found some old shed and spent the night there. It wasn't that bad. The early autumn weather was still warm. He sneaked home several times for food. He made sure it was late in the evening so nobody would see him, yet once a neighbor spotted him and, taking him for a thief, scared him away with his shouts. The man ran away from his own apartment. And so, a whole month passed. The tramp had no intention of ending the experiment. He got carried away. He'd never felt so free. He found two shabby blankets, a piece of mirror, a knife without a handle and an almost intact radio with missing batteries. His big discovery was a rocking chair he mended with some wire and never strayed away from. He even made friends with a real tramp who taught him how to find some food every day, though the man had brought some money with him. And so, day by day, the line between the experiment and the real life of the tramp faded away. He felt no inclination to go back to his previous life. He didn't see the point. He was living in another, yet parallel city.

Once he played the following joke. Or it wasn't really a joke, because he was almost starving. He went into a little restaurant on Slaveikov Square which closed 'when the kiosks opened,' as they used to say. Once he used to go there with a crowd of aspiring writers. So the tramp went inside and indeed everybody was there. He didn't flinch but headed straight for their table, took a chair and sat down with a polite greeting. Nobody recognized him. This restaurant was frequented by all kinds of bums, so nobody paid much attention. The waitress even brought him a fork and he calmly took a bite from the plate of his one-time best friend. Then he took an empty glass, poured himself some wine and made a toast to the whole group, ending it with a little quotation from Eliot, his favorite lines from *Ash Wednesday*:

> Because I do not hope to turn again
> Because I do not hope
> Because I do not hope to turn

And then he said something like: 'I drink to the fucking postmodern situation whose prophets I take you to be.' He knew those people well and he won them over immediately. He spent the whole night with them, eating and drinking all he wanted, he had fun, he watched them—deep in thought about their pudgy wives. He never turned right, though, because his ex-wife was sitting there (I didn't know he had had a wife, honest) and he was sure she had recognized him.

This is my idea so far. I don't know what will happen with the tramp in the end. It occurred to me that if I want the novel to turn out well, I'd also have to live as a tramp. Just for a couple of days.

that year many dogs were run over cats matted hair blood on the bushes tails in the gutters he moved in with emma with three aquariums fish breed easily die easily pigeons so many around the garbage cans i what don't eat them i can smell we are of the same breed season's greetings dogs are not allowed into the store salesgirls wanted clinton is leaving maybe whose is that girl no i don't want a home only a home toilet flyyyy flyyyy is your decision final smile please sokolovi bros get off from the cherry

A Final Epigraph

I'll become totally extinct
He told them
I'll become totally extinct
He told them
Like the dinosaurs

About the Author

Georgi Gospodinov was born in Bulgaria in 1968. In addition to *Natural Novel,* he is the author of two collections of poetry and one book of short stories. He is also the editor-in-chief of a weekly literary magazine published in Bulgaria and a professor at the New Bulgarian University. He lives and works in Sofia, Bulgaria.

PIERRE ALBERT-BIROT, *Grabinoulor.*
YUZ ALESHKOVSKY, *Kangaroo.*
FELIPE ALFAU, *Chromos.*
  Locos.
  Sentimental Songs.
IVAN ÂNGELO, *The Celebration.*
  The Tower of Glass.
DAVID ANTIN, *Talking.*
DJUNA BARNES, *Ladies Almanack.*
  Ryder.
JOHN BARTH, *LETTERS.*
  Sabbatical.
SVETISLAV BASARA, *Chinese Letter.*
ANDREI BITOV, *Pushkin House.*
LOUIS PAUL BOON, *Chapel Road.*
ROGER BOYLAN, *Killoyle.*
IGNÁCIO DE LOYOLA BRANDÃO, *Zero.*
CHRISTINE BROOKE-ROSE, *Amalgamemnon.*
BRIGID BROPHY, *In Transit.*
MEREDITH BROSNAN, *Mr. Dynamite.*
GERALD L. BRUNS,
  Modern Poetry and the Idea of Language.
GABRIELLE BURTON, *Heartbreak Hotel.*
MICHEL BUTOR, *Degrees.*
  Mobile.
  Portrait of the Artist as a Young Ape.
G. CABRERA INFANTE, *Three Trapped Tigers.*
JULIETA CAMPOS, *The Fear of Losing Eurydice.*
ANNE CARSON, *Eros the Bittersweet.*
CAMILO JOSÉ CELA, *The Family of Pascual Duarte.*
  The Hive.
LOUIS-FERDINAND CÉLINE, *Castle to Castle.*
  London Bridge.
  North.
  Rigadoon.
HUGO CHARTERIS, *The Tide Is Right.*
JEROME CHARYN, *The Tar Baby.*
MARC CHOLODENKO, *Mordechai Schamz.*
EMILY HOLMES COLEMAN, *The Shutter of Snow.*
ROBERT COOVER, *A Night at the Movies.*
STANLEY CRAWFORD, *Some Instructions to My Wife.*
ROBERT CREELEY, *Collected Prose.*
RENÉ CREVEL, *Putting My Foot in It.*
RALPH CUSACK, *Cadenza.*
SUSAN DAITCH, *L.C.*
  Storytown.
NIGEL DENNIS, *Cards of Identity.*
PETER DIMOCK,
  A Short Rhetoric for Leaving the Family.
ARIEL DORFMAN, *Konfidenz.*
COLEMAN DOWELL, *The Houses of Children.*
  Island People.
  Too Much Flesh and Jabez.
RIKKI DUCORNET, *The Complete Butcher's Tales.*
  The Fountains of Neptune.
  The Jade Cabinet.
  Phosphor in Dreamland.
  The Stain.
WILLIAM EASTLAKE, *The Bamboo Bed.*
  Castle Keep.
  Lyric of the Circle Heart.
JEAN ECHENOZ, *Chopin's Move.*
STANLEY ELKIN, *A Bad Man.*
  Boswell: A Modern Comedy.
  Criers and Kibitzers, Kibitzers and Criers.
  The Dick Gibson Show.
  The Franchiser.
  George Mills.

The Living End.
The MacGuffin.
The Magic Kingdom.
Mrs. Ted Bliss.
The Rabbi of Lud.
Van Gogh's Room at Arles.
ANNIE ERNAUX, *Cleaned Out.*
LAUREN FAIRBANKS, *Muzzle Thyself.*
  Sister Carrie.
LESLIE A. FIEDLER,
  Love and Death in the American Novel.
FORD MADOX FORD, *The March of Literature.*
CARLOS FUENTES, *Terra Nostra.*
  Where the Air Is Clear.
JANICE GALLOWAY, *Foreign Parts.*
  The Trick Is to Keep Breathing.
WILLIAM H. GASS, *The Tunnel.*
  Willie Masters' Lonesome Wife.
ETIENNE GILSON, *The Arts of the Beautiful.*
  Forms and Substances in the Arts.
C. S. GISCOMBE, *Giscome Road.*
  Here.
DOUGLAS GLOVER, *Bad News of the Heart.*
KAREN ELIZABETH GORDON, *The Red Shoes.*
GEORGI GOSPODINOV, *Natural Novel.*
PATRICK GRAINVILLE, *The Cave of Heaven.*
HENRY GREEN, *Blindness.*
  Concluding.
  Doting.
  Nothing.
JIŘÍ GRUŠA, *The Questionnaire.*
JOHN HAWKES, *Whistlejacket.*
AIDAN HIGGINS, *A Bestiary.*
  Flotsam and Jetsam.
  Langrishe, Go Down.
ALDOUS HUXLEY, *Antic Hay.*
  Crome Yellow.
  Point Counter Point.
  Those Barren Leaves.
  Time Must Have a Stop.
MIKHAIL IOSSEL AND JEFF PARKER, EDS., *Amerika:*
  Contemporary Russians View the United States.
GERT JONKE, *Geometric Regional Novel.*
JACQUES JOUET, *Mountain R.*
HUGH KENNER, *Flaubert, Joyce and Beckett:*
  The Stoic Comedians.
DANILO KIŠ, *Garden, Ashes.*
  A Tomb for Boris Davidovich.
TADEUSZ KONWICKI, *A Minor Apocalypse.*
  The Polish Complex.
ELAINE KRAF, *The Princess of 72nd Street.*
JIM KRUSOE, *Iceland.*
EWA KURYLUK, *Century 21.*
VIOLETTE LEDUC, *La Bâtarde.*
DEBORAH LEVY, *Billy and Girl.*
  Pillow Talk in Europe and Other Places.
JOSÉ LEZAMA LIMA, *Paradiso.*
OSMAN LINS, *Avalovara.*
  The Queen of the Prisons of Greece.
ALF MAC LOCHLAINN, *The Corpus in the Library.*
  Out of Focus.
RON LOEWINSOHN, *Magnetic Field(s).*
D. KEITH MANO, *Take Five.*
BEN MARCUS, *The Age of Wire and String.*
WALLACE MARKFIELD, *Teitlebaum's Window.*
  To an Early Grave.
DAVID MARKSON, *Reader's Block.*
  Springer's Progress.
  Wittgenstein's Mistress.

CAROLE MASO, *AVA*.

LADISLAV MATEJKA AND KRYSTYNA POMORSKA, EDS., *Readings in Russian Poetics: Formalist and Structuralist Views*.

HARRY MATHEWS,
The Case of the Persevering Maltese: Collected Essays.
Cigarettes.
The Conversions.
The Human Country: New and Collected Stories.
The Journalist.
Singular Pleasures.
The Sinking of the Odradek Stadium.
Tlooth.
20 Lines a Day.

ROBERT L. MCLAUGHLIN, ED.,
Innovations: An Anthology of Modern & Contemporary Fiction.

STEVEN MILLHAUSER, *The Barnum Museum*.
In the Penny Arcade.

RALPH J. MILLS, JR., *Essays on Poetry*.

OLIVE MOORE, *Spleen*.

NICHOLAS MOSLEY, *Accident*.
Assassins.
Catastrophe Practice.
Children of Darkness and Light.
The Hesperides Tree.
Hopeful Monsters.
Imago Bird.
Impossible Object.
Inventing God.
Judith.
Natalie Natalia.
Serpent.
The Uses of Slime Mould: Essays of Four Decades.

WARREN F. MOTTE, JR.,
Fables of the Novel: French Fiction since 1990.
Oulipo: A Primer of Potential Literature.

YVES NAVARRE, *Our Share of Time*.

DOROTHY NELSON, *Tar and Feathers*.

WILFRIDO D. NOLLEDO, *But for the Lovers*.

FLANN O'BRIEN, *At Swim-Two-Birds*.
At War.
The Best of Myles.
The Dalkey Archive.
Further Cuttings.
The Hard Life.
The Poor Mouth.
The Third Policeman.

CLAUDE OLLIER, *The Mise-en-Scène*.

FERNANDO DEL PASO, *Palinuro of Mexico*.

ROBERT PINGET, *The Inquisitory*.
Mahu or The Material.

RAYMOND QUENEAU, *The Last Days*.
Odile.
Pierrot Mon Ami.
Saint Glinglin.

ANN QUIN, *Berg*.
Passages.
Three.
Tripticks.

ISHMAEL REED, *The Free-Lance Pallbearers*.
The Last Days of Louisiana Red.
Reckless Eyeballing.
The Terrible Threes.
The Terrible Twos.
Yellow Back Radio Broke-Down.

JULIÁN RÍOS, *Larva: A Midsummer Night's Babel*.
Poundemonium.

AUGUSTO ROA BASTOS, *I the Supreme*.

JACQUES ROUBAUD, *The Great Fire of London*.
Hortense in Exile.
Hortense Is Abducted.
The Plurality of Worlds of Lewis.
The Princess Hoppy.
Some Thing Black.

LEON S. ROUDIEZ, *French Fiction Revisited*.

VEDRANA RUDAN, *Night*.

LUIS RAFAEL SÁNCHEZ, *Macho Camacho's Beat*.

SEVERO SARDUY, *Cobra & Maitreya*.

NATHALIE SARRAUTE, *Do You Hear Them?*
Martereau.

ARNO SCHMIDT, *Collected Stories*.
Nobodaddy's Children.

CHRISTINE SCHUTT, *Nightwork*.

GAIL SCOTT, *My Paris*.

JUNE AKERS SEESE,
Is This What Other Women Feel Too?
What Waiting Really Means.

AURELIE SHEEHAN, *Jack Kerouac Is Pregnant*.

VIKTOR SHKLOVSKY,
A Sentimental Journey: Memoirs 1917-1922.
Theory of Prose.
Third Factory.
Zoo, or Letters Not about Love.

JOSEF ŠKVORECKÝ,
The Engineer of Human Souls.

CLAUDE SIMON, *The Invitation*.

GILBERT SORRENTINO, *Aberration of Starlight*.
Blue Pastoral.
Crystal Vision.
Imaginative Qualities of Actual Things.
Mulligan Stew.
Pack of Lies.
The Sky Changes.
Something Said.
Splendide-Hôtel.
Steelwork.
Under the Shadow.

W. M. SPACKMAN, *The Complete Fiction*.

GERTRUDE STEIN, *Lucy Church Amiably*.
The Making of Americans.
A Novel of Thank You.

PIOTR SZEWC, *Annihilation*.

STEFAN THEMERSON, *Tom Harris*.

JEAN-PHILIPPE TOUSSAINT, *Television*.

ESTHER TUSQUETS, *Stranded*.

DUBRAVKA UGRESIC, *Thank You for Not Reading*.

LUISA VALENZUELA, *He Who Searches*.

BORIS VIAN, *Heartsnatcher*.

PAUL WEST, *Words for a Deaf Daughter & Gala*.

CURTIS WHITE, *America's Magic Mountain*.
The Idea of Home.
Memories of My Father Watching TV.
Monstrous Possibility: An Invitation to Literary Politics.
Requiem.

DIANE WILLIAMS, *Excitability: Selected Stories*.
Romancer Erector.

DOUGLAS WOOLF, *Wall to Wall*.
Ya! & John-Juan.

PHILIP WYLIE, *Generation of Vipers*.

MARGUERITE YOUNG, *Angel in the Forest*.
Miss MacIntosh, My Darling.

REYOUNG, *Unbabbling*.

LOUIS ZUKOFSKY, *Collected Fiction*.

SCOTT ZWIREN, *God Head*.